FIVE PATHS CROSSING

Jon Michael Miller

For
Beth Graham,
Jo Ann Costello,
Patricia Ann Ferguson,
and
Abram Rudisill.

Special Thanks to

Megan Shay,
Tom Russo,

And the entire Dunedin Writers Group, Dunedin Public Library,
Florida.

Queen:
Why seems it so particular with thee?
Hamlet:
Seems, madam? Nay it is. I know not *seems*.

... Act 1, Scene 2

FIVE PATHS CROSSING

1

"I'm very sorry to hear this, Dr. Shields," Luke's attorney said in the posh downtown Tallahassee office. "Did you get a second opinion?"

"I did, yes. It's clear, and coming on fast."

The silk suited lawyer nodded sadly. "And you wish to modify your last testament."

"Only slightly. I have four letters here, in sealed envelopes, addressed with your office as the return, to be sent when I'm gone. And as I've stipulated, in case you get any inquiries, no additional information whatsoever should be given."

"And do you wish to keep the university's academic scholarship fund as your sole beneficiary?"

"Yes. I have no remaining family."

"You don't want your name on a special endowment?"

"There is hardly enough for that," Luke commented dryly, thinking of years on endowment committees with deans scheming and scrimping to cover constantly escalating maintenance costs. "I'm not sure there is even enough to cover planting a tree these days, although that would be nice." He remembered lunches under a jacaranda, the blossoms carpeting the ground only a shade lighter than those dear, dear eyes. "A jacaranda would be nice. Let's do that."

The attorney smiled. "We'll add it as a requirement of the gift, with a small plaque."

"Not a requirement, just a request. And absolutely no plaque."

"As you wish, Dr. Shields. And when the time comes, you still want our firm, as your Executor, to be responsible for all decisions, financial and, uh, otherwise, as your living will decrees? Is that correct?"

"It is."

"All right. Just a few signatures. And may I say again how sorry I am."

"Thank you. Now, one last matter. And I'm sure everything we say here remains strictly private."

"Indeed. Attorney client privilege."

"Good. I have no intention of going through the deterioration of my mental capacity. Nor will I allow the absurd laws in this state to deplete all my funds in extending a useless life."

"My dear Dr. Shields..."

Luke held up a firm hand. "None of that. I am informing you. As soon as final details are taken care of, a few weeks, I'll make my exit in the manner of my own choosing. There will be no opportunity for sentimental arguments. I'm telling you only because your office will be informed. And above all, I want those letters to be sent."

~

Three weeks later, with Luke's final semester grades submitted, commencement participation completed, household items donated to the Salvation Army, book collection given to the university library, and the sale of his modest two bedroom bungalow closed, he made a purchase at a hardware store and drove his Subaru Outback an hour south to Cedar Key. There, he relaxed on the deck of a cheap motel. In a warm Gulf breeze, a cold glass of grapefruit juice in his hand, he watched his last sunset. It was especially dazzling, the red-gold orb sinking behind a line of clouds and then appearing once more below them before melting into the horizon.

Well into the night he received his wakeup call. He rose, gathered his few personal items, and drove back to the mainland then north along the coast. Eventually he pulled onto a dirt trail that led to a rough, seldom used shoreline where he came to a stop. Lighting his way with a flashlight, he opened his trunk and took out a length of tubing and a roll of duct tape. He slid the tube over the exhaust pipe, taped the gap tightly, and led the hose around to the driver's window, which he opened just enough. Then he taped up the four inch gap. Everything tightly sealed, he sat in the driver's seat, swallowed five OxyContin tabs with water from a plastic bottle, turned on a chant from Rig Veda, and started the engine.

He reclined his seat, lay back, crossed his arms over his chest, closed his eyes and inhaled deeply, regularly. Easily, he started thinking his mantra, allowing his thought process to slowly drift where it always had these final days – almost fifty years earlier to his dearest image – Paige's beautiful eyes.

Two days later the following snippet appeared in the *Tallahassee Democrat*:

> June 12, 2014
>
> Dr. Luke Marlin Shields, 72, was found asphyxiated in his car, 9 a.m., Wednesday, June 10. Levy County deputies were called by local fishermen to a remote stretch of beach near Cedar Key. Evidence obtained shows Shields to have been an emeritus professor of Asian Studies at Florida State where he taught and published articles for 32 years. A native of Lancaster, Pennsylvania, he earned a doctorate from the University of Delaware. No evidence of foul play was found, nor have any remaining family members been located.

2

June 20, San Francisco

When Dr. Jocelyn Consolo, psychiatrist specializing in women's issues, finished reading the registered letter she received from a law office in Tallahassee, she immediately directed her secretary to locate and dial the number of André Roulier in Lancaster, Pennsylvania. Jocelyn had not communicated with André in over ten years. They once were lovers, a lifesaving affair for her and a lifetime friendship. As director of design for an international tile and flooring company, he'd won numerous awards for his projects.

"Mr. Roulier is on the line, Dr. Consolo," Jocelyn's secretary said over the intercom. Jocelyn demanded professional formality in her busy office. She picked up.

"André!"

In a dusty artist smock, he munched a roast beef sandwich at the counter of his huge kitchen, a glass of fine Cabernet at the ready.

"Joss! Voice from the past."

"Yes, though I wish it were due to more pleasant circumstances. Luke has passed away."

"Heard. Got a weird letter sent by his lawyer in Florida. From Luke's will. *Upon his parting*, it says."

"The very reason I'm calling. I got one too. A kind of poem."

"How'd he die?"

"My assistant is checking as we speak."

"Seems he was a tad ticked off."

"Is yours the same as mine, titled 'Chicken Bones'?" Jocelyn asked.

"Different title. 'Tulips Turning.'"

"So, not the same. Does it happen to mention me?"

"Only about our fantastic summer together, Erica too. But seems he had a longstanding beef about my time with Paige."

"I guess it's his odd perspective on our prehistoric past. But it brought back our summer in an instant, nineteen sixty-seven. Yes, unforgettable, indeed. I always mark it as the beginning of my life."

"Yeah, but prehistoric is right," André said, taking another bite of his sandwich and talking with his mouth full. "Never was one to spend much time looking back. What's the use?"

"I wonder if Erica got one of these parting messages. Do you know where she is?"

"Last I heard, Seattle. Head of the library system, can you believe it?"

"She's come a long way, for sure," Jocelyn said.

"You know she turned to women, don't you?" André asked, slurping another swallow of wine. "Didn't surprise me. Would 'a done the same thing, if I'd been born female, but from the very start, no indecision about it."

"Yes, André. Aren't we all aware of your adoration of the female body? We are what we are, and isn't it fantastic our culture is finally waking up to that reality?"

"Never thought I'd see it, though. Even more incredible than having a black president."

"We've lived to see amazing things, André, and I agree, gay rights beats them all, more amazing than smartphones. I'll have my secretary try to reach Erica."

"Figure Luke included her in these writings?"

"Maybe. And where is Paige? Do you know?"

"Iowa, last I heard, with a meditation group. Levitate under a golden dome, I hear."

"Yes, hardly levitating, though. More like bouncing. They call it Vedic flying. I refer clients to Transcendental Meditation sometimes but only for stress relief, not for trying to defy gravity."

"Still saving lost souls, Joss?"

"It's my life. I'll keep going as long as I can make a difference. So Paige is in Iowa?"

"A while back, who knows? Always a searcher, always different." He rubbed the last crust of his baguette in the remaining beef juice and wolfed it down.

"Do you know her last name? It keeps changing."

"Last I recall it started with an *O* – Oswald, Osborne. William she called him. Wrote me a letter. Wanted me to take the meditation course."

"Amazing, André, how you keep in touch with your ex-conquests. Could you check her letter for her name?"

"Don't keep letters. Prefer looking where I'm headed, not where I've been. Haven't heard from her or Erica for a lot of years."

"I'll have my secretary do a search. Are you well, you old devil?"

"Hey, at eighty-one, well as can be expected. A touch of arthritis creeping into these old hands."

"Those hands are national treasures. You should leave them to science."

"Prefer to make use of them a little more before that." His tone softened. "So, do you remember?"

"For the *art* you create, you sleaze bag. For the art. Look, André, I want us all to get together again. Maybe in Luke's honor, or his memory, or just because ... I don't know why exactly. He said some things in this letter that made me think. I want us to meet back in Lancaster, where ... well, you know ... where it all started. How about over Labor Day? Would you be up for that?"

"With you, Joss, anytime, anywhere, of course. Anyone else included?"

"You, me, Erica and, Paige. If I can round everyone up. We visitors can book rooms in one of the town's quaint B & B's."

"You can stay at my place. Bought the Weaver Mansion on East James."

"My, my. That big home near the hospital? It was a wreck."

"A wreck no longer. Turning it into a gallery, if I hang on long enough. Plenty of room. Ha, sounds like a geriatric version of the Big Chill flick."

"At our ages," Jocelyn said, "far less drama I'm sure. Are you staying active?"

"How do you mean that?"

"How do you think, you fool?"

"I'm working on a sculpture garden for this place, chipping away at local limestone."

"Well, don't think it's going to be a foursome – you know, in *that* sense."

"Aw, shucks." He finished off his wine, wiped his hands on his smock. "Keep an open mind."

"Oh, be quiet. I've got to go. My nine o'clock patient just arrived. Strange poem from Luke. I'll be in touch."

After hanging up, Jocelyn instructed her secretary to find the numbers of Erica Grant in Seattle and of Paige or William Osborne, or Oswald, in Fairfield, Iowa. Maybe the search needed to be under Paige's maiden name – Flanagan. Jocelyn would reach them when she had a break.

A visit back home, she thought, reminiscing that life altering summer. And catching up. And finally, at last, getting a meaningful insight into Paige. So much time and effort with her, so little comprehension. Maybe even a glimpse into André –must be more there than seems. And then, a few things I need to resolve about myself. There are times in our lives, transitions, when we become what we are. That summer was mine. And Luke, poor, dear Luke was the catalyst. Won't it all be a trip?

~

Just home from a day of redesigning the rare books room of the city's public library, Erica Grant nuzzled her African grey, which cooed and cheeped, wings slightly spread with its vivid red tail on display. The window of the apartment faced across the sound, engulfed today in mist, the city's skyline not visible across the sound, the city's skyline engulfed in mist. When Erica's cellphone rang, she slipped the bird a marshmallow and picked up. After the surprise at hearing her old friend's voice, she addressed Jocelyn's question about a letter from Luke.

"Yes, Joss, I got one too. Yesterday. Had to sign for it. I'd almost forgotten about Luke. Surprised he even remembered me. My god, that was almost fifty years ago. What did he die of?"

"We're trying to find out. What's the title of your letter, or poem, whatever it's supposed to be?"

"'Brutal Purples.'"

"Was there bitterness in the tone?"

"More like disappointment. A lotta personal shit, though. He sounded like the wound was fresh. But damn him, he was the one who left me."

"André got a letter too. It started me thinking we should all get together. Lancaster, over Labor Day. André has a big house. Remember that old mansion on East James Street? We can stay there. Please, say yes."

Erica moved back to the cage, held out a wrist. The parrot climbed aboard.

"You, me and André?"

"Paige, too, if we can find her."

"Why her? Must we?"

"I know you two were always on different planets, but that summer was glorious, you have to admit."

"But Paige came in much later. I didn't meet her until I came west, must have been two years after."

"Do you still resent her for her thing with Luke?" Jocelyn asked. "I thought you'd been finished with him by the time the three of us were roomies."

"True, but she bugged me. So prim but such a slut."

"But, Erica, didn't we all have our breaking out bouts of sleeping around?"

"Not with all the hypocrisy, though."

"Maybe she won't want to come," Jocelyn said. "André says she's married, and ensconced in a cult. But I hope we can pry her loose for a weekend. It might be a little weird just you and I with André. And I'd bet my left arm Paige got one of these epistles too. I'd like to hear what Luke had to say to all of us."

"Yeah, Paige was into Luke big time. But the vibes between her and me were way out of synch."

"Don't you think the *three* of us would neutralize things with André?"

"You mean disorient him with herds and stripes, like zebras do with lions?"

Jocelyn laughed. "Quite an image, but, yes, like that, I suppose. And after all, at our age? Have you married, Erica? Now that it's legal?"

"No. I'm a solitaire. Spencer, my bird, is all the company I need." She kissed his beak. "Humans bug me. Living with one is out of the question. Are you still with Brien?"

"Lord, no. We divorced twenty years now, two grandkids with careers. I'm married to my practice."

"You really want Paige to come, Joss?"

"Yes, if she got a last message from Luke. I want us to talk about what he says. That whole thing appears to have been a life-long debilitating experience for him. His writing, whatever, really surprised me. And you're right about the fresh-wound sound of it."

"Shit, yes, Joss, it floored me too. But we were young. These things roll off us when we're young, don't they?"

"Didn't roll off Luke, apparently. Some people fixate on certain events, especially traumatic ones. Luke was the sensitive one among us, wasn't he?"

Spencer made a perfect imitation of Erica's cellphone ring.

"Is that an extra phone?" Jocelyn asked.

"No, that was Spence. He uses it to get my attention. Say hello, Spencer." She held the phone toward him.

"Hell-o," the bird said.

"Hello, Spencer," Jocelyn answered with a chuckle.

"All right, Joss, Lancaster, then. I can visit my daughter and grandkids, new great-granddaughter, too, if they'll see me, black sheep that I am. But I won't miss Paige if she doesn't show up. And let's make sure André doesn't get the wrong vibe, okay? I haven't been with a man since I discovered my true self in Frisco. Not even that charming bastard will tempt me at this point."

"At our ages, Erica? I'm sure that kind of temptation is long out of the picture."

"Speak for yourself, you old bat. And do you happen to be talking about the André we both knew?"

"Oh, you slept with him too?"

"Didn't you know that, Joss?"

"No. But somehow I'm not surprised."

8

"Yeah, no big deal. We were a pair of dumpees, saw each other for a few weeks, but it was after you left, and after Luke deserted me for grad school in Ohio – where he found his precious Paige."

"Okay, then, Erica. Back to our roots – Lancaster, Labor Day. I'll be in touch."

~

Paige Owens had just shifted from hatha yoga to pranayama when the phone rang. Normally she wouldn't have interrupted her routine, but it might have been her husband William calling. In tights and a loose top, she picked up and was shocked to hear Jocelyn's voice. After a few heartfelt preliminaries, Jocelyn laid out the plan for a Labor Day visit to the Keystone State.

"He bought a mansion?" Paige said. "I just remember that strange little place that used to be a candy factory."

"He's risen far above that dive. He's creating a gallery. We can all stay there. What's the title of Luke's letter to you?"

"'Futile Fragments.' How did he die?"

"We're doing a search. His attorney won't say."

"You know, Jocelyn, I live in a close community here, teaching classes, married, a tight regimen. Pretty hard to get away."

"All the more reason for a quick break to see old friends."

"*Complicated* old friends," Paige said, sitting back down on the thick foam in their 'flying room.' And I'll have to work it out with William. He's in London at the moment, won't like my leaving."

"London? Reason enough. You deserve a trip too. I know this is presumptuous of me, Paige, but you've been important to me, as was Luke and Erica. Please join us. Find a way, will you?"

"It's really that important?"

"To me, yes."

"Can you tell me why?"

"Let's call it some significant loose ends, piqued by Luke's message. He sent them to all four of us."

"It's just that I haven't been out of my pattern for a long time, and William will definitely object. His trip isn't social. He's meeting with our international board."

"Come on, Paige. Make it happen. I nursed you through a major crisis once, if you remember."

"Well, let's not make it due to a debt, which I agree I owe you."

"But we've been important to each other. Vital."

"Yes, that's true, Jocelyn. A tentative yes, but I'll have to work on it. Can't say for absolute sure. I'll let you know. You *do* realize, don't you, that Erica doesn't particularly like me."

"Come on, Paige, we're way beyond that kind of thing."

"I hope so," Paige said. "Poor Luke."

3

August 29, 2014, Lancaster, Pennsylvania

Jocelyn arrived first, from Philadelphia International. In her rental Toyota she phoned André, informing him that she'd just entered the city limits on East King. Five minutes later, imitating a traffic cop, he motioned her to pull into the drive, its wrought iron gates opened. In bibbed painter jeans with a black tee shirt and leather sandals, broad chested, in good shape, he appeared every bit the thriving artist. With a Ninja style headband, he wore his once shock of jet black hair, now gleaming gray, pulled back in a braid to his shoulder blades. A bit more than medium height, he sported a well-trimmed beard and mustache. His dark, slightly squinted eyes had their familiar subdued twinkle, his handsome face chiseled, more rugged than aged.

When Jocelyn got out of the car, they hugged tightly, affectionately.

"Positively dynamic with all that silver hair," Jocelyn said. "I expected you to be bald and potbellied like most aging profligates."

André chuckled. "And look at you. Devastating."

"A bit of help from a fine surgeon."

"Yeah? Me too. Some jowl reduction."

"Really, André? And not too vain to admit it. You've always been admirable when it comes to the truth of things. One of your most appealing traits. Rare in a man."

"One of yours too, my dear."

She took in the huge home, constructed of rust-red blocks, white woodwork and black iron fencing, shrouded by foliage and old maples. On the border of the historic downtown, the mansion had a long tradition – built by a prominent banker in the early 1800s, a Civil War hospital after Gettysburg, a meeting place for local magnates and political leaders, then like so many of the town's old grand residences, fallen into disrepair. The once magnificent homes on nearby North Duke Street had become mere shells for rundown apartments, a neighborhood to be avoided.

"I always forget how green Lancaster is," she said. "And how quiet. And amazing, André, that as cosmopolitan as you are, you've stayed here all your life."

"Job too good to leave. Philly and New York just train rides away."

"Never get a driver's license?"

"I did. Tool around town on a Vespa these days. A car's too much hassle. Cabs and mooching rides more my style."

He grabbed the bulkier of her two bags and ushered her into the house by the side door. Erica and Paige would arrive later, separately, the former from Harrisburg International, the latter at the city's small airport via Baltimore.

A vestibule opened into a living room with a polished wooden floor, a Persian carpet, numerous Roulier paintings on the wall, and Scandinavian furnishings that seamlessly fused the modern and the traditional.

"Magnificent!" she said. "Why am I not surprised?"

As of old, André took the compliment in stride. He carried her bag up the fluted spiral staircase and showed her to her room, decorated contemporaneously in contrast to the out-of-date radiators, high ceiling and tall windows with old wooden trim. Slants of sunlight slipped through the slightly opened plantation blinds. After he showed her the private bath, they hugged tightly again. He left her to freshen up after her transcontinental flight and two hour drive.

Jocelyn smiled, looked out the window at the wide, green maple leaves. She was slightly shorter than André but remembered looking taller with her teased hair way back when. In spite of his not being tall, he had something deeply appealing about him which pulled one instantly into his offbeat, idiosyncratic world. She looked around this splendid room.

Prominent above the king size platform bed was a massive impressionist like painting in multi shades of muted green, light horizontal streaks like moonlight across water, distant vertical lines like forest, sky above, frontal vertical lines resembling weeds with white buds of baby's breath.

He couldn't leave a corner bare, a wall without personality, an undistinctive space, including his own being. Immaculately groomed, he'd always delighted in current fashions but defied them just enough to stand apart, as though making fun of trendiness. He was more attractive now than ever.

She, however, had kept her hair blond and, these days, short, easy to manage. If André was avant garde, she was polished, refined, professional with just enough makeup to partially subdue the growing wrinkles her plastic surgeon had strategically left behind.

"We don't want you to look like Joan Rivers," he'd quipped.

When not working, which was seldom, she wore turtlenecks and loose slacks. Her profession had become her life. Affairs, once a constant, were now a nonpriority and at present nonexistent. Her facial expression had almost frozen into thoughtfulness, in listening mode. Her life struggle with her weight had resolved itself in a comfortable but stable figure bordering on stout, a look she'd come reluctantly to accept, no longer requiring the extraordinary effort of workouts and dieting. She'd freed herself from evaluating her appearance in the eyes of men. But in terms of professional standards, her first priority now, she measured up quite well.

She sighed. And here she stood once more in André's incredible realm. After soaking in the deep claw foot bathtub, she dried off with a thick towel, noticed just the slightest touch of jaundice in her complexion, stretched out on the knotted cotton bedspread and, relishing the coolness of the ceiling fan, drifted off to sleep.

~

Jocelyn awoke to the sounds of voices in the hallway, André's and clearly Erica's, as he was showing her to her room. Erica's laugh was unmistakable – and wonderful to hear, especially as it had occurred so rarely in Jocelyn's memory. Erica had kept her natural beauty well hidden beneath a stern, regal, judgmental expression that had masked her lack of confidence. Back then she'd felt inferior, Jocelyn eventually realized, due to having been a high school dropout because of pregnancy even though she'd later earned an equivalency diploma and had excelled in a secretary program.

Back in the summer of sixty-seven when they'd all met, Erica worked as a typist in a top rightwing legal office downtown on the then flourishing North Duke Street. But in spite of Erica's bootstrap success, Jocelyn came to know that her sense of lowliness had lodged itself deeply in her personality. Added to it was her guilt for having given up her out of wedlock daughter for adoption. As an adoptee herself, Jocelyn well understood the psychological complexity of parental abandonment.

But now, four plus decades later, Erica was laughing. She'd recovered, achieved, found herself. And of course, at the moment, André's presence, ever the genial host, could not be discounted.

Pulling on a thin, thigh high robe, Jocelyn looked out the window. A Yellow cab pulled up in front – no doubt Paige arriving.

Jocelyn opened the bedroom door just as Erica went into her room. In the hallway, André turned.

"Paige is here," Jocelyn said softly.

"Right. I'm playing the bellhop today."

A gong like doorbell sounded from downstairs. Of course, André would never use an ordinary tone. This one resonated like the entrance to a Thai ashram.

~

A yoga mat rolled under her arm, Paige waited uncertainly at the tall double doors with modern stain glass designs. She felt the distant strains of the bizarre ten months she'd spent in this small city, an abandoned refugee from her *thing*, whatever it might be called, with Luke Shields. Her subsequent deep training in Vedic philosophy caused her to reject the uncomfortable sensation as being absurdly far behind and irrelevant. She spent virtually zero time these days with memories of her long Siddhartha like and often deeply humiliating waywardness. She had arrived back here on this warm summer day because...?

Before she could finish the thought, the door opened and there stood André. Adorable André. Once lifesaving André. He stepped backward, a surprised look in his shining dark eyes as he took her all in.

"Bravo!" he said. "Stunning."

She felt her blush rise.

"And you too, André."

He stared at her. She laughed shyly.

"Well, might I come in?" she asked.

"Oh, right. Please." With a gallant sweep of his arm he gestured for her to enter.

"Are the others here?"

"They are. But who needs them?"

"You'd better stop that tone, André," she said, smiling.

"Not very gracious to ask the impossible of a man." He pulled in her sizeable suitcase on its rollers.

"I'm sure it's not the impossible, even for you."

"Long trip from the cornfields?"

"Des Moines, Chicago, Baltimore, here. Only fifteen hours."

"Must be exhausted. But don't look a bit of it."

"Looks can be deceiving. I did a lot of meditating along the way. But I could use a shower. And I need to stretch out the stress, then some rest on a nice bed."

"So, welcome to the Hotel Roulier. Saved you the honeymoon suite."

He led her to a back staircase and hoisted her bag upward in the narrow space.

"When did you take up bowling?" he asked, heaving the weighty suitcase. At the top, he added, "This is what they call an 'in-laws' apartment. So you get it all, can cook your own Ayurvedic meals if you like, make your own lettuce smoothies."

"I may have to unless we'll all share vegetarian cooking."

"Yes, so you said in your email. Told Caroline, the hired cook for the weekend. She'll find what you like, has your list. You remember the farmers' market?"

"It that still going on?"

"Hey, Amish country. All fresh, organic. Caroline is shopping there at this very moment. Aim to please here at the inn. No eggs? No scrapple and molasses?"

"Ugh!" Paige said with a smile. "Maybe the molasses."

He ushered her into the living room of a small apartment, windows facing the back, Lancaster General not far away, many trees and three story homes.

"We'll move the coffee table so you can spread your mat. Figured we'd all go out for our first meal together. Chinese, okay? Sure you can find something safely veggie there. Give you a wakeup call on your cellphone, three hours."

~

Loud chatter and hugs galore erupted in the spacious living room when the three women finally met – lots of "you look incredible" and the like as André stood by with a satisfied grin. Jocelyn wore a simple long sleeved, off white dress with a wide, gold choker and white pumps. Erica was much more casual in butterscotch capris and a buttoned cotton top. Paige, however, stood out in a bright purple and gold sari, a beige drape over the tightfitting *choli*. She'd parted her thick, wavy gray hair in the middle framing her model's face, gorgeous yet distinctive at once. She wore several gold bangles on her right wrist and Indian style sandals on her bare feet, pearl toenail polish, and a gold ring on the second toe of her right foot. She was the one who drew the oohs and ahs though she explained that her outfit was common fare in her present life, as it was for most of the women at the Vedic inspired enclave in Fairfield.

"There's nothing more comfortable," she said in her self-felt need for defense. "Why should I change my natural habit to fit in with this crazy world at large?"

"Stubborn," Erica said with a snicker. "Like the Amish."

Paige took the comment as subdued mockery, typical of Erica, especially toward her. Yes, picking up an earlier unfinished thought, Paige wondered why, exactly, she'd decided to leave her pure, *satvic* community to venture here. Certainly not because she wanted to. No, at first she'd declined and, at second, she had also. But Jocelyn had been extraordinarily demanding on the phone as was often her manner, as if ... as if this reunion was clearly the right thing to do. And after all, Jocelyn had saved her, had patiently tugged her up onto her feet after Luke had sent her to San Francisco from Columbus that bitterly cold first day of nineteen seventy.

Yes, Jocelyn had saved her, given her a new direction. Paige loved her for that, and ... owed her. So in the end she could not refuse her, even of this inexplicable get together, even of having to rehash Luke, of having to deal with his last words to her, received by registered mail. Following that phone conversation with Jocelyn had come the dreaded struggle with her husband William to permit her going out into the corrupted, polluted, Kali Yuga society. In spite of that stalemate, here she was.

Yes, here she was, back in this weary town, ordering cashew tofu (insisting on no fish sauce), salad with sesame dressing, steamed veggies and green tea. The age old Golden Wok on West King Street hadn't changed an iota, it seemed, from nineteen seventy-one. The others ordered cocktails, Tsingtao beer, spareribs, and a variety of meat dishes on a roundabout platter, André speaking to the server, whom he seemed friendly with, in perfect Chinese and wielding chopsticks as naturally as a native.

André. What a wonder in his mandarin tunic, and the small touches of personal adornment like the tiny gold carpenter's screw in his left earlobe, the strange Samoan like tattoo on his right forearm, and the odd musky timber scented cologne he wore. And of

15

course, that confident, all accepting grin highlighted by the devilish gleam in his dark eyes – even in his early eighties, a gem of a man.

Wishing this were their departure meal and that the upcoming weekend was now behind them, Paige listened to the catch up conversation among the other three, some of which facts she already knew. Jocelyn had earned a summa cum laude doctorate from U. C. Berkeley and established a thriving practice in a government supported program for abused women. It made complete sense – Paige, herself, having been Jocelyn's first patient back when Jocelyn was working from only pure instinct and sisterly compassion.

And Paige knew, also, of Erica's thing with Luke and her struggle with sexual identity. But she was surprised that Erica too had become an academic with a Ph.D. in library science. And as for André, what was there to know? As unique as he was, he'd been as stable as the Northern Star, yet in his style and in his art productions, a constant astonishment. Paige watched his tanned, rough, thick hands as he handled the chopsticks, hands she'd come well to know, and his merry eyes always masking a wink, ever playful, without self-consciousness, certainly free utterly of regrets and introspection. How could anyone be farther away on the spectrum from Jocelyn? How would he ever participate in the upcoming Jocelyn led examination of Luke's parting thoughts?

"Come on," he said to Jocelyn, "eat up, girl. Plenty left."

"I've learned to control my appetite," Jocelyn answered, "or I'd be a blimp by now. And please don't call me *girl*. Don't you know that's become a sexist term?" She winked.

He bowed his head. "I do beg your pardon, Madame."

"Twenty lashes," Erica said.

~

"You're not eating very much, Joss," André said again.

"Not very hungry this evening," she answered. Worried that Paige was being left out of the conversation, she turned to her. "And Paige, what do you do every day in that meditation community of yours?"

"Yeah," Erica chimed in, "sit around all day contemplating your bellybutton?"

"I teach, do some administrative work at the school."

"You teach lit?" Erica asked. "Like you used to do with Luke in Ohio?"

"No. After my master's in Vedic Studies I earned a doctorate in Sanskrit. That's what I teach."

"Sanskrit?" Erica scoffed.

"Yes, that's right."

"So you're into that meditation stuff hook, line and sinker," Erica said. "Sanskrit, Vedic Studies, Indian clothes, no meat. The Kama Sutra too?"

"It's hardly fair, Erica," Jocelyn interrupted, "to ask Paige to explain her belief system in this informal setting."

"Yeah," André said. "She can give us the rundown later. Maybe teach us some postures."

Jocelyn turned to Paige. "Could you write something down in Sanskrit? Of all the languages, I think it's the most beautiful on the page. Here, use this napkin." She found a pen in her purse and handed it to Paige, who wrote something and handed it to Jocelyn, who put on her glasses, had a look, smiled and passed it to André, who did the same and passed it to Erica.

"What the hell's it mean?" Erica asked.

"Can you translate it for us?" Jocelyn said.

Paige read and then recited the meaning – *One who keeps good friends will benefit and live in peace* – they all politely applauded the sentiment.

"How appropriate for the occasion!" Jocelyn said.

"Sounds like something from a fortune cookie," Erica quipped.

4

Faint Miles Davis jazz in the background, they gathered in the chat alcove of André's big living room, with cognac and strawberry cheesecake – warm milk and honey for Paige. A roughhewn wagon with patina rusted wheels served as a coffee table. In pairs they sat on two facing beige couches with lots of colorful pillows. A fireplace was bordered by a limestone frame with André's carved Inca inspired designs. From the ceiling hung a whimsical mobile of intricate insect figures in variously colored, glinting foil – a grasshopper, a praying mantis, a walking stick, a dung beetle, several others – all drifting about in the minimal breeze of the A.C. On one wall hung a giant painting of distorted, red, flame like stems resembling sumac trees as if viewed from a speeding vehicle. On the opposite wall, white plantation blinds opened to the darkness of a side lawn. A rattan mat covered the white planked floor.

All of them settled in, Erica wanted to know why, precisely, Jocelyn had brought the four of them back together.

"It must be something more than your devotion to Luke's memory," Erica said. "Sure, we all cared about him, eons ago, but frankly I think his unloading these letters on us shows passive aggression, like a kid dropping a stink bomb and running away to..."

"To his death," Jocelyn said. "And no surviving family except, in his mind, maybe us."

"How do you know there was no family?" Erica asked.

"My secretary found a small article in a Tallahassee paper that said so. He asphyxiated himself in his car, no surviving family."

"Jesus Christ!" Erica said with annoyance. "What was he up to with this stunt?"

"I thought he died of cancer or something," André said. "Wow. So he offed himself."

"Yes. On a remote beach, the article said, found by fishermen."

Paige was drying her eyes with a napkin.

"I'll try to explain why I wanted to meet you all again," Jocelyn went on, her lower back beginning to throb. It was an hour past her usual bedtime. "And I wouldn't say it's my devotion to Luke except he was part of the beginning of things for me, I mean of real life instead of teenage naiveté. Sometimes it's a benefit to have a close look at one's source."

"Is this meeting free psychotherapy for us?" Erica asked. "After the price I paid for the airline ticket, you'd better not hand me a bill."

Coming out of their sad spot, they smiled.

"No psychotherapy, Erica, I promise. But I think the fact that each of you agreed, and took some pains to get here, tells us something."

"That we love and respect you," Paige offered.

"Okay," Erica went on, "that established, truly, now what's on the agenda, Joss? I'm sure you have one all typed out."

They laughed lightly.

"Nothing for tonight. It's just the deepest pleasure I can imagine to see you all again. Everyone well and thriving."

"Except Luke," André said.

"Yes, and did everyone bring his letter, as I asked?"

"You mean *insisted*," Erica said.

Having long ago abandoned the value of examining the past, Paige was silent, finished drying her eyes. She'd indeed brought her letter from Luke. Looking back on all of that was like recalling a past life – which was, according to her own present belief, as utterly useless as rummaging through garbage. When once asked why we can't remember our past lives, Maharishi had answered with his characteristic flippancy: "Because we'd all be too embarrassed." She was here for one reason only – her commitment to Jocelyn. As far as Luke was concerned, she felt only sadness and shame. But she'd known him more intimately than anyone here, of that she was certain.

"The agenda?" Erica said.

"I want us all to see everyone's letter. I'd like us all to share."

Oh, no, Paige thought. *Please.*

"I'm sure we can send lovely André out tomorrow morning to make copies, so that we can read them together, try to figure out what was going on in Luke's mind. And what it means to all of us."

"Must we, really?" Paige asked. "Can't we just enjoy the present, being together?"

"Yeah," Erica added in rare agreement with Paige, "why dig up the past, almost half a century?"

"Because it's the source, the beginning, isn't it? Except for André who was and always has been André?"

The three women seemed in agreement of this latter fact.

"Can you deny, Paige, that it was the beginning?" Jocelyn asked, shifting to comfort Paige back into the group. Jocelyn had taken only two polite bites of her dessert but swallowed all the brandy from her snifter.

Paige felt herself coloring. "It *was* the beginning. I can't deny that. But I'm far away from this kind of self-searching."

"Do it for me then," Jocelyn said softly, looking at Paige and playing a card she hadn't cared to. But she was dedicated to this process. And if Paige wasn't, she was wrong even if she had to be pushed out of her spiritual Iowa cocoon for a brief time. How often in her practice had Jocelyn dealt with denial!

Paige smiled gently. "All right, but only for you, Jocelyn."

"Thank you, Paige." Jocelyn yawned. "So why don't we all give our letters to André, and I'm sure he knows a place to make copies."

"My office," he said, pointing to a door across the wide space. "Won't have to go anywhere in the morning unless Caroline forgets the donuts. Can do the printing right now."

"How many pages do each of us have?" Jocelyn said. "Mine is five."

"Mine, too," Erica said.

"Six," added Paige.

"Only two and a half," André said. "Guess he let me off easy."

"Well, that's a lot of pages," Jocelyn said, "so let's wait until the morning. What will we do for breakfast? Go out somewhere?"

"No need," André said. "Caroline will be here at eight, delightful woman, certified chef, had her own restaurant in Barbados. And knows about your requirements, Paige, so no omelet for you. She even knows how to make *ghee*."

"What the hell is ghee?" Erica asked.

"It's what comes out when you strain melted butter," André answered. "Learned that on Wikipedia after I got Paige's wish list."

"What's it used for?"

"Search me, didn't read that far. What's it used for, Paige?"

"Cooking. Less fatty. Good for one's skin and hair."

"It's sure working for you," André said.

"Okay, excuse me," Jocelyn said, "but it's been a dreadfully long day with a delightful conclusion. I'm thrilled we're all here, and thanks to dear André, could we be any more comfortable?" With effort and wincing at a sharp pain, she rose to her feet. "I'll bid you all good night."

"Me too," Paige said, rising also. "After I do the dishes, André."

"Not on your life. They can wait till morning. Caroline cleans up with the best of them."

"Then I'll die of guilt. Let me rinse them off, at least."

"And let's give our letters to André," Jocelyn added, "so he can print them up. Then after breakfast tomorrow we'll read them together and have a talk. I'm sure our discussion will prove quite thought provoking."

"And pretty damn humiliating," said Erica. "If mine's typical, we should all be ready for hairy details, warts and all. Good that we all once shared so much together."

"We'll help with the cleanup," Jocelyn said to Paige.

"No, thanks. You're hurting. Go to bed, Jocelyn."

"I'll pitch in, I guess," said Erica.

"And I'll follow you for your letter, Joss," André said. "Save you a trip up and down the stairs. Maybe tuck you in."

"Now André," Jocelyn said smiling. "Spry as you may be, or may think you are, there will be none of that."

5

With the dishes and glassware washed, Paige went upstairs, pulled Luke's letter out of her suitcase and took it back down to André, who was seated at the glass desk in his office warming up the printer. She handed him her pages.

"What do you think of all this, André?"

"Whatever. Back that summer Joss made me learn pinochle. *She*'s the item of interest, not the activities she comes up with. When you and I were together, didn't I put up with your meditation breaks?"

"And did so with utter graciousness. Until just this moment, I had no sense whatever of your having *put up* with them."

"Life's to enjoy, right? And what's more enjoyable than a beautiful woman, whether at cards or sitting cross legged on the floor with her eyes closed. And now, a modern miracle, I seem to have three."

"No one steady? To be jealous of all this?"

"Muriel took this 'opportunity' to visit her sister in Maine."

"Oh, so there *is* someone. I was sure of that." She sat on a sleek Scandinavian easy chair.

"So, Paige, you went all in for the meditation stuff. As I remember, you left me for a training course somewhere in Italy."

"Fuji," she said, swiveling her chair back and forth. "A divine little mountain town with mineral baths."

"And after that, only one letter, recruiting me for Transcendental Meditation."

"Out of a sense of duty, André. I knew you wouldn't go for it. You – sitting still for half an hour twice a day? – I doubt it. But when one has found an answer, you want to share it with those you love."

"My favorite book is *Zen and the Art of Motorcycle Maintenance*, though. Give me credit for appreciating the philosophy, at least."

Paige smiled. "Yes, but this is a practice, not a philosophy. It's experiential, not intellectual."

"Well, if it leads to celibacy, forget it."

"Celibacy?" She stopped swiveling. "Where did you get that idea?"

"In the letter from Italy, you mentioned that women and men stayed in separate areas. I made a mental note of that. But knowing you, I figured you somehow found a way to cross the barriers."

"Oh. Separated only for teacher training, so we could stay on point. We did find our chances, though. And married couples lived together. Maharishi greatly encouraged marriage, for the sake of decency, he said, particularly for representatives of the teaching. He, himself, was a life celibate."

"Like the Pope?"

"Yes, but not a requirement for his teachers. Guys had to cut their hair, too, and wear coats and ties. But meditation gives one more vigor for whatever activity." She paused as if catching herself. "Sorry, André, I know we're not here to convert anyone to anything. But I didn't want you to think meditation dampens one's libido. Quite the opposite. I'm not leading a nun's life."

"Yeah, that was hard to picture. Good." He smiled. "And I'm doing fine in the vigor department." He slipped a packet of papers into the feeder. The printer whirred.

"Yes, I sense your energy, André. You don't seem to have slowed down a bit. And you're still you, and we all love you for not having deviated from your natural path. In my community we call it one's *dharma*."

Erica showed up at the door with her letter. "Here this *thing* is. I'm far past baring my soul like this. It's damn demeaning if you want the truth. If it wasn't for Joss, forget it."

"Is she all right?" André asked.

"Why do you think she might not be?" Paige said.

"Didn't eat much. Extra tired."

"A long day," Erica said, dropping her packet onto the desk, "but I'm dying for a cigarette. Still indulge, André?"

"On occasion. We'll have to use the gazebo. Took us forever to get the tobacco smell out of these walls."

"I'll see you in the morning," Paige said, rising, not having had a cigarette since before her trip to Fuji when she'd smoked with André. And not only tobacco.

~

22

Erica followed André out a back door to an octagonal structure with a tarp covered hot tub surrounded by foliage, quiet in the sultry August night except for the chirping of crickets. André offered her a cigarillo, holding a pack he'd taken from his desk drawer.

"No thanks. I'll stick to my Virginia Slims."

"Was dying for a big fat Cuban with that Courvoisier."

"No way with this group," Erica said, lighting up and extending her lighter flame for André.

They exhaled smoke in unison and stretched out on loungers.

"What's going on with this literary conference, André?"

"Joss is a trip. And this is one hundred percent Joss. I can dig it because I dig her."

"Do you like Paige?"

"Sure. What's not to like?"

"Well, she's a beauty all right, but all this bullshit—ghee, yoga, Indian clothes for Christ sake. The only thing missing is a red dot on her forehead."

"Looks damn good in a sari. I'll focus on the aesthetics, if you don't mind. You're standing out in that department too. Go with the flow is what I say."

A dog barked in the distance.

"Did your letter from Luke mention you and me, André?"

"No. Not a word. Not a comma."

"Did Luke know about us? It was just a few weeks after he left for Columbus, and I knew he was ending it even though he didn't say so."

"I never told him about those lovely few weeks. Luke know about you and Randy?"

"Might have suspected. I just wasn't very monogamous back then."

"Still have those pictures Randy took in his studio?"

"God, no. Where does that kind of ancient stuff disappear anyway – class rings, concert programs, nude pictures?"

"Gorgeous. You stark naked, swirls of smoke, lots of expression. Luke ever see 'em?"

"He liked them, appreciated fine art."

"But never knew what else happened during that shoot?"

"Hell, no."

"Figured you just lolled around in your birthday suit being photographed? Luke was smart but a little unaware."

"He did two great things for me, though," Erica said. "Got me out of Ayn Rand and into working for Bobby, and pushed me into higher education. I owe him that. But he was a real coward about breaking up with me. Just drove off for Ohio and left me hanging. I'd forgotten all about it until I got this damn letter, or poem, whatever it is. But, André..."

He let a few smoke rings out, settled back in his chair. "Yeah, Erica?"

"I have the feeling we're headed for a confessional. No need for them to know about you and me, is there? Joss already knows, but not Paige. Unless it comes up in these letters. Can I have a look when we're back inside?"

"I think Paige knows about us, Erica. You never told her? When you were flowerchildren together in Frisco?"

"No, and Paige and I lived in the same apartment with Joss, that was as far as it went. Your description of our *togetherness* is anything but accurate."

"Now wait, Erica. Didn't mean it like that."

"Okay. Good." She sat up, leaned forward. "What made you think Paige was susceptible to something like that?"

"Don't know. She seemed pretty receptive to experimenting back then. But Paige's knowing about us did happen to come out during my time with her."

"So you spilled your guts? Not like you, André, to discuss your other lovers. Never did with me."

"Paige brought it up, if I remember."

"What the hell? Well, I did mention it to Joss during her cross examinations. So *she* must have told Paige."

"Anyway, kiddo, Paige knows. What's it matter?"

"Let's go in. I want to see those other letters."

Back in André's office, Erica leafed through all the documents as he clipped them together in packets.

"Good," she said. "Strange, they sound like letters but look like poems. Nothing about you and me, André. So can't see it coming up, can you?"

"I won't mention it. No shame in it, though."

"Jesus, André, you slept with all three of us, and here we all are. Incredible. Look at what Luke says about me here." She handed him her pages, leaned over his shoulder. "These lines."

He read, chuckled. "Yeah, pretty explicit."

"God damn it. And he has to mention that, and we're all going to read it and talk about it. Fuck!"

"Doubt Luke thought Joss would organize a cross continental convention about these poems. And I'm sure we don't have to *discuss* these details, Erica. Hey, you had talent with a man. Probably transfers to women as well, since you changed teams, as Seinfeld would say."

"Ha ha, André."

"Hey, we five were all pretty interconnected, weren't we? An incestuous bunch. Anyway, Erica, if there's anything we all haven't known about each other, I doubt there will be after this weekend."

"André?"

"Yes, my dear Erica?"

"I want to ask a small favor of you."

"Ask and it shall be shall be given."

"I want to redact those couple lines, okay?"

"Redact?"

"Yes, before everybody sees them. Your printer has a scanner function, right?"

"State of the art."

"So I can scan the letter, save it as a document, delete that crap, reprint it, and who'll know but you and me? So, no need to bring those completely extraneous issues under discussion. Just let me take care of it, okay?"

"No problem, but I'm surprised you're so sensitive about it."

"Who wouldn't be?"

"Yeah, I guess so, but..."

"Jesus, but what?"

"You've always been so openly you, Erica."

"Well, I guess some things change, don't they?"

"Seems so. Why not just tell Joss you don't want to do this exercise?"

"I did, several times but she was really insistent."

"That's her all right. But she's not your boss."

"But she helped me when I was with her in Frisco. Took the time to listen to me talk things out, to accept my 'changing teams,' I mean feeling normal about it rather than disoriented. She made a huge difference in my life, like she liberated me from the stupid strictures of society."

"I see. So now she's calling in the debt. All right, but if you take out those lines, she and Paige might notice."

"How?"

"Luke wrote this stuff in poetry form, with verses, same number of lines in each one. Knock out some lines, and it might be obvious. And anyway, isn't redacting, like, blacking parts out. That only makes people more curious. Like the transcripts of the Nixon tapes. That's not the same as eliminating the lines altogether."

"Forget the semantics, André. If anyone is counting the damn lines, I'll let Luke's lousy poetic ability take the blame. Just let me do it."

"Sure. Be my guest. Anyway, Erica, how'd you ever develop your truly mind-blowing skill in the sack? Just a natural gift? Which, incidentally, I remember quite vividly."

"Shut up, André. Holy hell!"

6

Well after their nine o'clock breakfast time, Jocelyn wandered into the big kitchen, yawning. She nibbled at her island omelet as bright eyed Caroline, a plump, busty Caribbean American, hustled about in an apron over a stretch halter and a long skirt. Her head was covered by a lime green bandana knotted in front. Large hoop earrings accentuated the darkness of her skin. She beamed at the compliments about her cooking.

The kitchen smelled of bacon, toast and coffee, and gleamed of stainless steel, with a diner like breakfast bar and a round wooden table where everyone was seated. After their meal, the foursome regrouped in the living room alcove, the pages of Luke's correspondence in hand.

"Feels like English class at Lancaster High," André said. "Gonna be a quiz, Joss?"

"Indulge me," she said. "I, for one, can't wait."

Erica groaned. Paige blushed.

Caroline had set the coffee table with mini cups of custards, bowls of pineapple chunks, mango, and papaya, and a decanter of Blue Mountain coffee. With little crosstalk the group shuffled their papers restlessly.

Jocelyn knew the others were reluctant, only following her lead, paying back whatever favors they might think they owed her. So be it. She would force them through this. She wanted to resolve something from her distant past, to find closure. Everyone knew she could be unabashedly selfish when she wanted something – and in this case she was even willing to reveal her own darkest secret.

"So where do we go from here?" Erica asked. "If you're the same old Joss, I'm sure you have it all mapped out."

"Let's look at these writings one by one, read them aloud. André can start by reading Erica's, then Paige can read mine, then I'll read Paige's, and last, Erica André's."

"How'd you figure all that out?" Erica asked.

"Just trying to organize things. We won't get through them all this morning anyway, maybe only yours. We have two whole days, no hurry."

"But why?" Paige pleaded.

"Yeah," echoed Erica. "Why?"

André beamed as if this was going to be one helluva party. "Should we fasten our seatbelts?"

"One reason why," Jocelyn went on, "is that I want to know if collectively, we damaged Luke's psyche. I mean, why did he hang onto all these feelings so long then drop them in our laps like this? It's remarkable to me that we four kept in touch with each other, more or less, but not with Luke. He seemed out of the circle, but now suddenly, as apparently his last act, he's back in. I want to deal with it. And I want your help."

"Hardly his *very* last act," André spoke. "But enough said. Let's get this show on the road."

"But why start with me?" Erica asked.

"Because," Jocelyn answered, "you were the first among us to be close to him. I came in later, then André, then Paige."

"Damn it, Joss," Erica said, "I hope this shows you how much we love you."

"Thanks, Erica. And let's everyone follow along as André reads. This will be a kind of forensic analysis. Let's find out exactly what was on Luke's mind."

In twos, they sat on the facing sofas separated by the morsel laden coffee table, on one side Jocelyn in slacks and a long sleeved turtleneck, Paige in a blended pastel Indian kurta with white leggings; and on the other side Erica in denim shorts and loose tee shirt and André in linen beach slacks and a tropical shirt, silver hair pulled back. They arranged papers to find Luke's letter to Erica.

"Ready?" Jocelyn asked.

27

They nodded nervously except for a merry brightness in André's dark eyes.

"And let's allow André to read the entire thing through without interruption, to capture the whole flow. Then we'll come back and work our way through it, okay?"

They nodded as if submitting to Jocelyn's authority. André began, stumbling, as if not used to reading aloud.

BRUTAL PURPLES
From Luke Shields to Erica Grant
Upon my parting

Paige saw you as a rival with whom,
She said, she couldn't deal.
The danger of those heart revealing
Confessionals as prelude to much more,
At once creating bond and sowing

Seeds of later strife. I spoke too much
Of you, and too intensely, with no idea
What Paige and I would come to be. I
Was in quandary at the time,
Having left you for Columbus, feeling I'd

Abandoned you, tormented by the guilt.
I even asked Paige what to do, to which
With eyes gone gravely sad, she asked
Me, simply, what I wanted. Unaware
I wanted her, I answered that I didn't know,

That I was torn. To help, I thought, she
Asked me everything about you. I told
Her first of what we'd shared, our picnics
Down along the river, Laurel Run and
Pequea Dam, summer Susquehanna, that

We'd float on inner tubes from trucks,
On lazy currents, you, André, Joss and I,
Passing doobies, stark-ass naked, grinning
At the wisps of clouds. That we'd throw
A Frisbee in the little park on Chestnut Street,

Your long strides smooth as a gazelle's,

Long hair whipping, golden in the evening
Sun, then, exhausted, lounging on a path side
Bench as fireflies began to flicker all
Around, giddy children racing by on

Roller skates. I even said how in our post
Orgasmic silliness we'd whirl our cigarettes
In fiery arcs to make red pinwheel circles
In the dark. That was our bond, of course,
In bed, from that first night, you on vengeful

Rebound from petulant Doug, I searching
For a thrill. You gave me that in spades...
... I wasn't used
To girls like you, meeting and going to bed almost

Simultaneously. So, irresistibly attracted,
Part of me was equally repelled because
Of how I'd typed you from the start,
Disreputable, uneducated, loose, available
For raunchy copulation but not to

Worry much about, a late night drop-in,
An early morning exit, not much more.
Until the caring came, my urge to nurture,
To force you to reveal your inner self,
To pry away the layers you'd built up

In self-defense. Your father's drunken
Visits to your bed, you mother's string
Of dope fiend lovers in the house, your violent
Brother's run-ins with the law, your countless
Boyfriends since age twelve. And certainly

Your deepest pain, surrendering little
Lori to adoption. All of it to activate
My savior side. Not that we discussed it
Much with your inveterate distrust of words.
For hadn't words betrayed you all your life,

Your father's, brother's, many partners' words,
So many promises gone unfulfilled? No surprise
We fell apart, words so vitally significant
To me. I told her, to assuage my guilt, I'd

Been of help to you. Never that you'd asked

For help or would have. You wore your
Independence like a badge of courage, purple
Heart for all the damage you'd incurred.
Still, I pulled you up a notch or two, reading
Parts from Shakespeare plays on

Sunday afternoons, arguing against your Goldwater
Politics, enrolling you in courses at the college,
Pushing you to practice Spanish. At my
Urging you even tried out for a play, won
The part and went on to dazzle sleepy Lancaster in

Ibsen, Beckett and O'Neill. Yes, I took some
Credit for all that. But though I wanted to,
And tried, I was never fully able to commit.
And felt the sin, I told her, of throwing you
A lifeline and then withdrawing it, too

Selfish for the task of loving you, too weak
To cut the bond with clarity, and leaving you
With nothing but my vague departure. How
Could I blame you for your bitterness? What
Comfort could you feel to hear my leaving

Wasn't easy, that I drove in tears along
The Turnpike, through the tunnels, half way
To Columbus, felt Glen Campbell's
Famous ballad each and every mile, your getting
Ready for your day, each step in your routine

As close to me as emptiness. I'd broken off
From something truly sweet, a reach across
Vast gulfs by two greatly different souls who'd
Tried their best to care. I simply wanted more,
I said to her, a deeper bond, a natural loyalty,

A union without effort. I hoped with all
My being that such a fusion lay ahead for me.
"You think a bond like that is really possible?"
She asked. And that's exactly how it did
Become for me with her. Not when I was

Telling her of you, but later as we became
Enmeshed. That process had almost been
Completed when I came back to you that
Christmas holiday. But not enough to stop
My seeking mercy in your arms. You sneered

Your condemnation, flaunted your new lovers,
An aging poet and a black renegade. Nonetheless,
We shared a tab of acid, listened to the Beatles
Sing of blackbirds, revolution and raccoons,
Until you taunted me with sex and finally...

... A metaphor of control, without doubt,
Otherwise so absent from your life. This your
Primal fantasy, you once confessed, someone
You admired or with power over you, so

Abjectly in your service. You could be
Stimulated to completion by the very thought.
How gratified you must have felt when we
Last met in San Francisco at Jocelyn's, by
Then my transcendental love affair gone

Hopelessly awry. Sweet revenge, I'm sure,
To have been a wedge between us, the irony
Your never having been a threat to her at all.
At any rate, you did seem quite content,
Self-satisfied as we rode in virtual silence

To the end of Geary Boulevard to share
With hippie throngs the sunset from
Seal Rock. The evening glow had
Seemed to wash the city's pinks and yellows
Clean, the savage truth between us

Much too evident for words. Instead,
We merely viewed a daily miracle,
A common crimson disc descend from
Sight behind a slowly turning planet,
Streaking brutal purples on a silent sea.

~

"Whew," André said, dropping the pages on the coffee table.
"The end."

"So, what now, Joss?" Erica asked with a scowl. "Let's do this. As a poet, he gets a D minus from me. Damn."

"All right, Erica, his poetic ability isn't our interest. At least he took the time to frame his ideas aesthetically."

"Sure, okay. What now?"

7

His reading chore completed, André used a toothpick to spear a chunk of mango which he popped into his mouth, grabbed the bowl and sank back on the sofa as the group relaxed, all wriggling, changing postures.

"And let's remember," Jocelyn said, "we're all friends here. Hardly a secret among us, okay? Some of that must have been rough on you, Erica, but we know you're strong."

"Yeah, right."

"So, since he's addressing you, who's the *she*?"

"Our Hindu princess on your left," said Erica grumpily. "There was no rivalry whatsoever on my part. Luke and I were over and done with. So he liked *her* more than me, so what? My relationship with him wasn't that serious anyway, and we both knew it. I moved on to other guys at the time, and he moved on to Paige and talked to her about me, who cares?"

"Past partners can be serious competitors, though," Jocelyn said, "never *entirely* out of the picture. What's curious to me is that he apparently used you, Erica, as part of his come-on to you, Paige."

"I don't think that's quite fair to say," Paige said, squirming. She clutched a pillow to her chest.

"Why isn't it fair?"

"We were only getting to know each other. Yes, we were talking intimately, but only as friends. He knew I was married. But we made each other laugh. And talked about serious things too."

"So," Jocelyn said, sitting on the edge of the couch, her back as straight as a cellist's, "he felt he could speak freely because you were unavailable? Is that what you're saying?"

"Probably. We'd started having lunch together in the Student Union. We liked each other, wanted to talk. He told me about Erica, and I told him personal things about my marriage."

"How'd you first meet?" André asked, devouring more mango pieces.

Jocelyn warmed at his coming magnanimously to her aid in the discussion.

"How we met isn't in the poem," Paige said. "It's immaterial."

"But there's a starting point in every romance," André stated professorially. "Like the universe – a big bang."

"Be serious for once, André," Jocelyn said, turning back to Paige. "So when *did* you first notice Luke. Do you happen to remember?"

"Actually, I do, if you need to know."

"Please."

Erica sank back, happy to be off the hook for the moment.

"All right," Paige began, still clutching the pillow. "Luke and I were both new graduate assistants in the English Department, and it was our first orientation meeting. We were introducing ourselves, and this tall, good looking guy was on his feet, raving about his senior English teacher in high school. He was praising this teacher's technique, then seemed to catch himself, realized there was no real point to what he was saying, stopped, turned red, and said something like, 'And if it wasn't for her, I wouldn't be standing here today.' He sank back down in his seat, and the whole place cracked up."

"Why?" Erica asked, her legs crossed at her knees and one bare foot flapping nervously.

"It was just funny, him having lapsed into unneeded, maybe even inappropriate sentimentality, then realizing it and being able to laugh at himself. I liked him immediately. We all did."

Jocelyn felt a stab of pain in her lower back, shifted in her seat. "Do you remember what happened as things progressed?"

"Not exactly. Our orientation group met every week to go over lesson plans, and he'd been a teacher for a while, in high school, for a draft deferment. I'd been teaching too, in Columbus, but the others were brand new and we helped them out with advice." The pillow had become a shield against the world. "I just saw him, listened when he spoke, and liked him. But aren't we getting far away from the poem?"

"That's okay by me," Erica said, pouring more coffee from a decanter into her mug, one of a set fired and glazed by André.

"Right," said Jocelyn. "Paige, when did he start telling you about Erica?"

"When we started having lunch together."

"How'd that begin?" André asked, the fruit gone.

"Well, actually, I asked him to, but ..."

"But, what?" André asked. "Come on, Paige, Joss says we're all friends here, remember?"

Again, Jocelyn warmed in gratitude.

"Almost forgot we're all friends," Erica said. "I can't imagine why it slipped my mind."

"Okay," Paige went on. "It was weird. He had an office with a friend of mine, Fred, from undergrad at OSU. Sara, *my* officemate, had a crush on Luke, used to tell me all about her innocuous run-ins with him in the hallway, on the elevator, you know, and Sara tried to seduce him one Friday night at his place, and it didn't go well, and I was a little ticked off at him but also pleased, oddly, that he'd rejected her."

"Ah ha," André said. "The plot thickens."

"Not the time for teasing," Jocelyn said. "Please, go on, Paige."

"Well, I bumped into my undergrad friend, Fred, and wanted to have lunch with him to see if Luke had said anything to him about Sara, but Fred was on his way to class and told me Luke was upstairs in their office, said I should go up there and talk to *him* if I was so curious. I did go up, poked my head in, saw Luke at his desk, and I didn't want to be too obvious, so instead of just being direct, I asked if Fred was there, that I wanted company for lunch. Of course, it was obvious Fred wasn't there, and he said Fred had a class, which of course I already knew, and that he, Luke, would tell Fred I'd dropped by."

"Not sure I quite followed that," André said.

"You seem to have a very clear memory of this particular incident," Jocelyn noted. "Even after all this time."

"I do, ever since. Luke has always been not far away from my thoughts, actually. And it was one of my more embarrassing moments."

"So," André said, exchanging eye contact with Jocelyn, "you were scheming, is that the point?"

"I was hoping he'd fall for my little stunt and offer to join me for lunch, but he didn't. I just stood there, mortified as he got back to his work. So I left. I probably recall it because that was the point I realized my feelings were getting complicated."

"In what way," Jocelyn asked, battling the pain her back.

"I guess what I realized most was, well, that I'd been jealous of Sara."

"Why, if she was failing with Luke?" Jocelyn asked.

"It was her freedom, to run around chasing her feelings, following her impulses, highs and lows. I felt trapped in my marriage, like, I don't know, like the fun of being young was over for me. And I felt relieved that Sara had failed with him, and I respected him for turning down something frivolous. Most men would have taken advantage of the situation."

"Not me," André said, grinning.

"Yeah, right," Erica countered, still pleased that she was not part of the conversation.

"So," André said, "when did Erica arrive in the courtship proceedings?"

"Okay, sorry," Paige answered. "And it didn't start out as courtship. I just want you all to know, Luke and I happened slowly."

"Not frivolously," Jocelyn noted.

"Correct. But in spite of my better judgment, I did a bit more scheming. A small group had started, Luke the center of it, for lunch at the Union, six or seven, talking about teaching and lit, and I edged my way into that group, and admired him more and more. He was funny and smart, and very nice looking. His hair longish, but not hippie-ish, and he wore wire rimmed glasses in vogue back then. One time we ended up together at the usual table, no one else, just we two, don't know why. And then we talked. You know, about our histories. Nothing flirtatious. My rings were on obvious display."

Erica stood, stretched restlessly, looked up at the insect mobile circling randomly.

"I know," Paige said, "I'm taking a long time. We're almost there. I can stop."

"No," Jocelyn said, "please continue."

"Yes," Erica agreed, shifting her attention to André's large painting, "please do."

"Okay, if you need to know. I wanted to have more private conversations, but there were always others around. Sara told me that instead of going out to the High Street bars on Saturday nights, Luke spent his time in the library. He was very serious about his studies, which I respected. So one weekend when my husband was training with the National Guard, I went to the library too, and we were the only ones there, and ended up at an Italian restaurant having dinner and wine. I asked him about Sara, why he didn't get involved with her, and that's when Erica came into the picture."

"This should be fascinating," Erica said. She sat down again, cross legged, attentive, foot moving to an invisible beat.

"He said, like in the poem – which is hardly a D minus, Erica – that he was confused, about you, that is. That he'd left you back home, things unresolved, cared for you but was looking for something deeper, etcetera, just as he wrote, about a higher kind of love, soul mates, which being, I don't know, more grounded, I guess, I wasn't sure even existed. I knew in my marriage, after the honeymoon wore off, love seemed a lot of work, a daily grind."

A calico cat with a red collar wandered into the gathering.

"Okay, everyone," André said. "Meet Cinnamon."

The cat jumped up beside him and settled onto his lap, everyone smiling. André stroked its chin.

"My daughter rescued her from an alley fight, nursed her back to health, and I'm the lucky recipient."

The group settled in for more of Paige's tale.

"But," Jocelyn said, "Luke believed in something more idealistic?"

"Yes, in something really special. Our conversation was getting heavier, and I wanted to keep the spotlight away from my marriage, so I kept asking him questions. And I could tell he was really mixed up about his feelings for you, Erica, and it seemed like he needed to talk about it with someone."

"Did he actually mention Erica's mixed up past?" André asked, "like in the poem? Which, since we're handing out grades, I thought was pretty damn good, at least a B."

"No, not much about her past," Paige said. "I'm sure he didn't mean for all of us to know those details, didn't realize we'd share these letters communally."

"Exactly right," Erica said, glaring at Jocelyn.

"Yes," Jocelyn agreed, meeting Erica's eyes. "Thank you, Erica, for submitting to this." She turned sideways to Paige. "So I guess his concern about Erica added to your admiration, right?"

"It's always stirring when a handsome man takes you into his confidence, isn't it?"

"Absolutely," Jocelyn answered. "You're not on trial here, Paige."

"And I'm sure he wasn't doing it as a *come-on,* Jocelyn." Paige's pillow seemed to have melded with her being, her hands wringing each other in front. "He was just revealing himself to someone he appreciated. We were on the same level, a few years older than most of the new teachers, both bearing the battle scars of high school classrooms. He made no signal whatever that he was noticing me romantically. I'm sure of that because I was probably watching for those signals. I was grateful later that he hadn't. So if I was appearing approachable, he wasn't taking notice."

"*Approachable?*" Erica said. "Jesus, you were throwing yourself at him."

"No I wasn't, Erica. I was getting to know him, and vice versa, nothing wrong with..."

"I need a smoke," Erica said, rising.

"A break is a good idea," Jocelyn said. "Please, let's be civil. We're getting somewhere, I think."

"Not sure where, exactly," André commented, setting Cinnamon onto the floor mat. "But I could use a smoke too. Anyone care to join Erica and me at the gazebo? Jocelyn, you used to smoke like a fire engine."

"Yeah," Erica added, rising. "You used to hold those Tarytons in your lips and make sucking noises when you puffed."

"Sucked your thumb too," André said. "Like you were two years old."

"No need to go there," Jocelyn answered, struggling to her feet. "I stopped all that oral fixation forty years ago, when Berkeley banned smoking in classrooms, thank god."

"You were a really sexy number," André said.

"That was when most women had nothing else going for them. And you really must refine your language, André."

"You mean be more politically correct."

"At least to recognize women as more than objects for your pleasure."

"Why would I ever want to do that," André muttered as they dispersed.

8

In the gazebo Erica and André lit up as they had the night before. On both sides of a meandering path and shrouded by greenery and flowering shrubs, oddly shaped sculptures in gray stone spotted the backyard landscape.

"Learn anything vital to your existence?" André asked.

"Not vital, but ever since I read Luke's letter, or poem, I *did* realize how deeply he felt about me. But back then I was really pissed at him. He just joined the long shit list, the same as all the other men I'd been with."

"Me included?"

Erica took a puff, smiled. "No, not you, André. I doubt you're on anyone's list, politically incorrect or not. From you, I got exactly what I expected, no more, no less, and all sweet."

They smoked in silence.

"Anyway," she said, "when are we going to use this hot tub?"

"How 'bout our afternoon analysis session?"

"Joss won't go for it. She seems all covered up."

"She can sit on the edge, dangle her big toes."

"And Paige? Do Hindus wear swimsuits?"

"If we need them at all."

"Jesus, André. We're way past that. No need to stare at each other's wrinkled butts. I'm so glad I deleted those lines. No one seemed to notice."

"Paige is painting a nice picture of old Luke, don't you think? Not like he was on the make."

"But she certainly had the hots for him."

"Sure she did but, Erica, no need to be in her face about it."

"She just annoys me coming off so prissy, when ... oh, never mind. You're right, I'm just not a very civil person."

Erica kicked off her flip flops. They smoked.

"But," she said, "looking back from this long distance, I can say Luke was a good guy. It wasn't his leaving me that ticked me off, it was the way he did it – and the fact that it's what all the men in my life did."

"And, since that, the women?"

"I'd hardened about love by that time. I never saw myself in a traditional union with a woman. Gay marriage? Any marriage? No, not me. I'm a lone wolf. I foraged the gay bars down in the Castro District, took what I wanted and moved on. Anyway, so when it comes right down to it, I have no complaints about Luke. We were young. Who among us knew what we were doing?"

"Joss might have," André answered. "Ever see her confused about anything?"

"Demanding, yes. Confused, never. She's a control freak, don't you think?"

~

When the group reassembled in the chat alcove, minus the feline, Jocelyn suggested they get back to the poem. "He paints a picture of that summer. Is his description accurate?"

"Pretty much," André answered. "Nice times, skinny-dipping, all of it."

"Not hippies," Erica said, "but hip. Lancaster's vanguard of the sexual revolution."

"Erica, do you think it's fair," Jocelyn asked, "for Luke to say that sex was the bond between you two?"

"Fair? Okay, at first. But I agree now that he cared about me."

"And who was this *petulant Doug*?"

"*Petulant* is exactly right. He was a thrill seeking biker with long dark hair and beard. Wore shades even at night. Loved speed. Loved screwing. Totally disloyal, doper – hard stuff, too – needles. I never shared that. I hate needles. Doug was an emotional rollercoaster, classic bipolar. He came and went, literally."

"Tell us how you and Luke got together," Jocelyn said.

Erica heaved an annoyed sigh. "All right. Anything to hurry things along. Doug was friends with a group of college types. They hung out in an apartment downtown on East King. Beer and singalongs – Kingston Trio, stuff, Peter, Paul and Mary. Drinking games, too. Luke was one of the lead singers, nice voice, a teacher at the high school, suits and ties. One night I went there with Doug. Damn if he didn't pick up some hippie chick and leave me alone. As things were winding down at the party, Luke asked me if I wanted to go to the diner for a piece of pie. I was really fuming about Doug. So I said okay. We ended up at Luke's apartment, in bed."

"After the pie?" Andre asked.

"We skipped the pie."

"Love at first roll?" he said.

"Christ no, I hardly knew the guy, just that he was the type that would piss Doug off. Anyone in that vast category would have done."

"How do you feel about Luke's description of you?" Jocelyn asked.

"Fair enough. I was no paragon of virtue. Never was. But those were the days, weren't they? And I'm sure Luke didn't expect anyone but me to read this D minus poem."

"A striking beauty," André said. "Still are."

"Shut your sweet yap, André."

"And was it like Luke says here?" Jocelyn continued. "He came and went, like Doug."

"Yeah, as the spirit moved him, like all of them. He'd call late. If I was alone except for my little girl, I'd say okay. Lori was with me then. She was four, which is why guys came late, when she was asleep."

"And petulant Doug?"

"Oh, Doug blew his own brains out one night, under a tree on a back road out near Lititz."

"God!" Paige said.

"Over you, Erica?" Jocelyn asked.

"No one knew why. I'm certainly no *femme fatale*. It was just like Doug to do something violent and stupid."

"Being with Luke must have been quite a contrast," Jocelyn said, shifting to ease the pain in her back.

"Yes. Luke was calm, nice, respectful. He helped me get through giving little Lori up. I don't think he played around on me. Then when Lori was settled with my aunt, he moved in with me. Nice times. Not thrilling, but nice."

"That word *nice* keeps coming up," Jocelyn noted.

"If the shoe fits," Erica said.

"He *was* nice," Paige added.

"I think we can all agree how nice he was," Jocelyn said. "Which is one reason I called this meeting. He's worth our attention, now, sadly, that he's gone."

"Doubt he thought these letters would go this far," said André, attacking the hitherto untouched bowl of pineapple.

"I dearly regret he died feeling hurt by all of it," Jocelyn said. "I guess we don't think very much about the feelings of nice people."

40

"Yes," Erica added, "let's call up all the nice people we know and tell them how nice they are." She grabbed a toothpick and speared a chunk of fruit. "Don't hog all the food, André."

"So, Erica," Jocelyn went on, "do you agree with Luke's claim that he helped you elevate your life?"

"No doubt. He opened my vision to my hidden potential. And, boy, was it hidden! And not only him, but you and André too."

"But mostly Luke."

"Yes. We lived together. He got me into the *New York Times* on Sunday mornings. We watched *Star Trek* together, talked about diversity, life on other planets. If God exists. We read plays. He convinced me to try out for the Drama Society. He was the kick in the ass I needed."

"And did you use your sex appeal to get revenge?" Jocelyn added. "As he says about that Christmas break?"

"Yeah, what about that acid trip?" André asked.

"I don't remember it much," she said, munching, "just that the White Album had come out. We tripped and went to bed. It's so great on acid. But, yeah, it was my M.O. to use sex to get even, so I'll plead guilty."

"'Metaphor of power,'" André quoted.

"Ancient history." Erica gazed upward. "Forgive me, Lord. Are we almost through with me on the witness stand?"

"All except," Jocelyn proceeded, "that last reference to Seal Rock."

Erica wiped her lips on her forearm. "You remember I came out to visit you in Frisco, right?"

"Of course. You were on the cusp and needed a little nudge to get over to the other side where you belonged."

"And thank you for that nudge. I haven't looked back for a second. And Luke was visiting you too. I guess he'd gone out west with Paige, and she'd left him for someone else. It was awkward as hell. He was hurting but trying to keep it together, being nice to me, feeling an obligation, I think, so he took me for a ride in his VW van like we had something to talk about, which we didn't." She speared another pineapple chunk, held it in front of her lips, waved it slightly as she spoke. "Whatever feeling of revenge I may have had was gone. He is right, though, when he says I felt a nasty pleasure in his thing with Paige having fallen apart. But we didn't talk much at all, just rode, watched the sunset with all the flowerchildren, went back to your place, Joss." She popped the fruit into her mouth. "Next day he was gone before I woke up, headed back home to Lancaster. I remember he seemed really messed up. I'd never seen him like that."

The attention shifted to Paige, who averted her eyes, the pillow now in her lap, her hands crossed on top.

"Not my finest hour," she acknowledged. "Talk about ambiguous endings."

Erica rose, opened the slats of the blind and peered out at the greenery.

"Before we leave Erica's poem," Jocelyn said, "we need to return to the opening lines, bringing you back in, Paige. So when Luke was telling you about Erica, did you really see her as a rival? Were you taking notes, so to speak, that affected your later relationship?"

"Not at first, but I did see you, Erica, as a powerful person in his life. I wasn't very experienced then, a virgin when I got married. Of course, one can do a lot of things before the big moment, which I did plenty of, but I'd only gone all the way with my husband on our wedding night."

At the window Erica faked a gag.

"It's true, I swear. Luke sounded as if he'd had lots of experience, and you too, Erica. I felt intimidated, and later when my moods turned dark, I did throw those images back at him, especially what he'd told me about seeing you over Christmas break. Even though I'd slept with my husband Ted that whole week."

"He says here," Jocelyn said, finding the lines, "that you two were *almost* enmeshed at that time, meaning you hadn't yet slept together?"

Paige blushed. She'd blushed more already this weekend than she had in the last thirty years.

"That's right. We'd begun meeting at his apartment just across from campus on High Street, a dingy little place with a brick fireplace. He had a picture of Erica on the shelf, in the woods with a garland in her hair – I thought you were really beautiful, Erica."

"Sure, sure," Erica said, still peering outside.

"I did think that, for what it's worth. Luke and I only *talked* until that afternoon before he left for break. Actually I was ready the first time he invited me over, expected it. Only conversation though. But the day before break, incredible tension in the air – I remember it so clearly...

...flashback to December, 1968

Her coat off, beads of melted snow in her hair, she sat on the ragged sofa in Luke's shabby, dim apartment. Tomorrow he'd be on the road back to his home in Pennsylvania. He was in the tiny kitchen, tall, good looking, pouring bourbon into glasses with ice. He came back, handed a drink to her, sat down close, took a sip.

"So," he said. "Here we are."

"Yes, and tomorrow you'll be with Erica again."

He nodded grimly.

"Have you figured that out?" she asked.

He looked at her. At this point, after all their private talk, she didn't care about Erica, wanted only for him to take her in his arms at last.

"It's complicated with Erica now," he said.

"Is it?"

"Don't you know that?"

"Complicated – why?"

"You."

They stared at each other.

"Look, Paige. We've become ... close. I'm feeling something deeply about you."

"Yes. And I for you."

"We've got to think about this."

"I suppose so."

"We're at a crossroads here. What we do will change things. Maybe, when I get back, you should invite me home for dinner, and I can meet your husband, and..."

"Oh, no," she said without thought. "I don't want you to meet my husband."

She was flooded with desire, him so close to her, eyes so serious, his faint scent.

"We've got to consider the consequences. This isn't simple. Others are involved."

She only looked into his eyes.

"I know you're not into casual affairs. You're not that type, not a cheater."

Again, she waited.

"So, if we do this, we must be sure."

He stood up decisively, tall above her.

"We have some time now, time to think. I don't want you to be hurt, don't want your reputation ruined. This is something rare, precious, not to be treated lightly. It's a ... Jesus ... a commitment, with ramifications. I'm sure you see that, don't you?"

She stared up at him. He was right, but at that moment she didn't want him to be.

"I'll go home to Lancaster," he said. "In three weeks, we'll meet again. Meantime, we'll decide how we feel and what we want. So, man oh man, you'd better go now, Paige. I'm sorry, but I'm on the verge of doing something I shouldn't. And you shouldn't either. I'm sure you know that."

Their eyes locked a long dreadful moment. Yes, he'd go home, she thought bitterly, get hooked up with Erica. But he was right. He was decent. Saying nothing, she set her glass aside, the drink untouched, and stood up, an exile from her raw desire. He was actually serious about their parting at this moment. He helped her on with her coat, opened the door. But she was unable to step through to the hallway. They stood at the threshold. She looked up at him.

Then he grabbed her to him, bent down and kissed her. A hungry kiss, long, full of meaning, of everything, it seemed, that they'd been holding back.

~

"Sounds just like Luke," Jocelyn said, "ever the deep thinker."

Paige peered at her clasped hands in her lap.

"It was a kiss I've never forgotten. Powerful, passionate. And ending far too soon." She shook her head side to side, took a breath, as if she'd been back there.

Looking up, she said, "Anyway, so we thought about it over the break, when he was *abjectly* with you, Erica, and when he got back he told me what had happened but that it hadn't been the same with you as before and he was sorry, that he now knew he was in love with me, and I was feeling that about him too. So we went to bed. It was – profound."

"Congratulations," Erica said. "You were the big winner."

"I didn't mean it like that, Erica."

"Hardly matters now."

"Luke told me about that doorway kiss," André said.

"He did?"

"Yeah. I remember now. He dropped by for a visit that Christmas. I used to cut his hair. Said he met someone, a married woman, and when I said, oh, the best, a horny housewife, he got ticked. Said, no, not that, much more than that. And when I asked what about the little issue of her hubby, he said something that stuck with me all these years."

"And what was that?" Jocelyn asked.

"He said, that when two people find such a feeling, others just have to try to understand. Mistakes need to be corrected. But when the Red Sea parts, you got to go through. Said that those who understood this kind of feeling, they'd be hurt but would back off. Those who didn't would just have to deal with it because when something that fantastic comes along, it can't be sacrificed. It's what life is all about. That's the gist of what he said, anyway."

"You never believed in the Grand Passion, did you, André?" Jocelyn asked.

"Not really. But Luke was way past any arguing about it."

"Sex as purely recreational?"

"Even more fun than white water rafting. And much safer. Luke didn't realize he was headed into life threatening rapids."

"Yes," Jocelyn said, "the ones right in front of Niagara Falls. Okay, then. Wow! Luke called me around that time, Paige. Told me he'd found IT. I remember that call because he sounded so euphoric."

"That's exactly the right word," Paige said. She sighed, shrugged, added sadly, "*Euphoric.*"

"He said on the phone he'd met the most beautiful creature in the universe."

Paige looked at the others, smiled meekly.

"So," Jocelyn said, "okay. Any more questions for Erica? It *is* her poem, after all."

Erica, sensing this trial was coming to an end, closed the slats and plopped back down beside André.

"Your distrust of words, Erica," Paige said. "Is it still your feeling? If so, all this talk must be killing you."

"Luke was right on about that. The distrust lingers even now, I'll admit, even though I work with books and texts day in, day out. And glad my time on this hot seat is almost over. But I'd just like to say that I owe a lot to Luke. Wish I'd known it then. Wish he were here so I could kiss his cheek."

"Or share a tab of acid?" André asked.

Erica grabbed a small cushion and hurled it at him.

9

For lunch André suggested they sojourn eastward on Route 30 where in many years past they delighted in raiding the smorgasbord at Miller's Amish Restaurant. In her rented Camry Jocelyn drove them through heavy Labor Day traffic. Tourist traps and outlet malls now lined the once rural Lincoln Highway, obscuring the verdant farmland. At the restaurant Paige found plenty of fresh organic veggies and fruits. The chatting was often interrupted by someone rising for seconds or thirds though Jocelyn's soup portion was trifling, a buffet lost on her mild appetite. Erica gorged on the chicken pot pie and eventually returned with a plate of shoofly and lemon sponge pie, homemade peach ice cream and tapioca pudding. In former days, Luke among them and Paige not, Jocelyn had led the feasting.

"I move we meet at the hot tub this afternoon," Erica said on their way back on a country road where they could take in the beauty of the land. They had to slow down behind a line of traffic trailing an Amish horse drawn buggy. Jocelyn maneuvered among the recent droppings.

They saw whole Amish families in the fields, harvesting hay, hand gathering it into bales which they tied and heaved onto oxen drawn wagons. Along the way they passed an occasional roadside food stand at an Amish farm.

André seconded the Jacuzzi motion.

"I didn't bring anything for a hot tub," Paige said.

"Nor I," Jocelyn echoed.

"So you two party poopers can just enjoy the shade like old fogies," Erica said.

"Or we could all *not* wear anything?" André suggested.

"For comic relief?" Jocelyn answered.

"Did you guys really go skinny dipping together?" Paige asked.

"Indeed we did," André said.

"Didn't you and Luke?" Jocelyn asked.

"Yes, but just we two. Oh, except..."

"Don't leave us hanging," André said. "Except when?"

"We went to Woodstock. And the second night there, in the river. But..."

"But what?" Jocelyn said.

"The others were strangers, and we were very high, and it was dark, except for some torches on the bank. Oh, then there was one time when we were alone on a beach at Big Sur."

"I was at Altamont," Jocelyn said. "What a nightmare! Anyway, Erica, as an old fogy, I'll take you up on enjoying the shade. Yes, we can talk outside. Why not?"

"We can stop for swimsuits, ladies," André said.

"Not me," Jocelyn said, "but maybe for Paige. How do you manage to stay so svelte, you and Erica?"

"Running, lifting," Erica answered.

"Hatha yoga, the right food," Paige added. "But I'll join you, Jocelyn, in the shade." She took in the view. "This countryside is so magnificent, like Fairfield except with hills."

~

Erica in a modest one piece, André in Corona trunks, his silver chest hair gleaming, the pair sloshed in the foaming, chemical scented Jacuzzi waters while the other two in shorts sat on the edge, dangling their feet and ankles. Soon evident to Jocelyn was that the sound and warmth of the whirlpool would not be conducive for thoughtful discussion, so she asked André to turn off the jets though he and Erica stayed in the tub with some gleeful leg wrestling. An iron fence and thick foliage gave the large back yard privacy, and they all had glasses of strawberry lemonade prepared and delivered by the ever grinning, long skirted Caroline.

Eventually with all their papers arranged, Paige began reading the letter/poem Luke had instructed his attorney to send to Jocelyn.

CHICKEN BONES
From Luke Shields to Jocelyn Consolo
Upon my parting

Of all you were to me, culmination
Was as refuge for my beloved Paige,
Sent your way, to San Francisco for
Reform, reclamation of my unity with
Her in your long trusted hands.

Yes, you and I'd been lovers several
Years before, between quite casual
Sheets, seduction then your habit, like
Your diet pills, despite immersion
In the passion of your life, an idle hour

And I would do to pass the time. Okay,
Certainly, with me. You were, then,
After all, a bombshell blond, buxom
To every man's distraction, with the added
Intrigue of an intellect, as though you dyed

Your hair a cotton candy yellow and piled
It high with spray only in order to defy a stereotype.
A look that did the trick with Reverend
Anthony. Impossible to ignore for him,
You surely were, mingling at Unitarian teas

In miniskirts, dark lined eyes a doll-like
Blue, your social conscience so aroused by
Brilliant, witty sermons. So how could I accept
Your dreadful claim? Was it my impulse
To assume responsibility or the simple fact

I cared? And so conveniently in possession
Of a friend named Goloff, in med school, who
Knew of someone who would do the
Operation for a mere two hundred bucks.
That was an oddly forbidding trip to Wilmington.

Yes, surely, we were friends. How else
Could we have felt so close in the face
Of our unresolved divergence? No prochoice
Movement then, no sympathetic throng
To bless what you were resolved to do.

True, I'd fought against it, suggested
Marriage as our duty, which you laughed
Away as an absurdity. No, I was not
A candidate for that. So we found the
Faceless building and to escape a drizzle

Lost ourselves in matinee, Cary Grant
Courting Audrey Hepburn in gay Paree.
Then I waited, fraught with worry, as
You went inside and climbed the dimly
Lighted stairs. The city street was lined

With sapling sycamores, early April pale
In green. Streetlights glimmered in the
Rain. When you finally came back, you limped
In pain, both hands to your side, but with your
Problem solved. We rode in eerie silence, home.

You held my hand, insisted we'd done right.
Such vacant hours after that, my hovering

48

Around you like a nurse, companion in our crime.
When Tony left, your affair found out,
Ignominiously transferred to Buffalo,

You lost another life within you. So,
I was all you had, my role, I knew, as Tony
Said to me in private, just to keep you here.
Broke your door in once to see if you were
Still alive. But you weren't there. Your

Little Lime Street flat its usual mess, bed sheets
Strewn with chicken bones, vanity in disarray,
Television on. Two days passed before you called
From André's, who'd picked you up, you said, at
Wanamaker's fragrance counter. Lesson for me

In feminine adaptability, suicide so quickly
Lost in lust. But, oh, such deep relief
To hear you laugh again. I'd found Erica
By then, and there we were, we four, reflecting
In our laughter luxuriant Lancaster County June.

We roamed the world in tandem, Marx Brothers'
Flicks high on marijuana, watermelon and Chianti,
Pinochle hilarity, Horse Inn clams and steak,
Lazy Susquehanna in canoes, chasing Frisbees down
In Musser Park. André's shed in alleyway, half

Nest, half gallery, ladder-trapdoor passage,
Incomprehensible contraption sculptures.
Your preacher's virtual opposite, you told me once,
As though raw hedonism can obliterate a moral
Force. Freed by pleasure from life's

Greatest loss, tragedy a blessing in disguise.
It should have served me warning for
A later trust. You left us then, in August,
With surprising ease, for a windy city on a lake,
Solid in your sense of self, and even mussed

Meticulous coiffure confronting Mayor Daly's
Thugs. Erica and I watched your riotous throng from bed.
King and Kennedy were shot. The war raged on.
André with another girl, of course. And

Jon Michael Miller

On a warm September morning I fled from

Erica, onward to Columbus, soon to find myself
Swirling in my own Grand Passion. I wrote to
You, in California then, exuberant, of Paige.
Who could better understand? Who'd been there
With more intensity? You knew, didn't you,

Of perfect synchronicity, utter sensual glee,
The unity of two souls blending, thoughts of
Nothing else but finally glimpsing one another
Down a crowded street, across a room, professor
Droning on, interminable minutes until a joyous

Fusion, single breath. You'd told me once,
"Spirits reuniting from across a universe." Yes,
You knew. I needn't ask, not even now, for
That was what defined you, what you were.
You were, no matter how you dealt with it in

Loss, a casualty of that. And I become, in cold
Ohio campus walks, not yet a casualty, a sharer
Of your secret, immutably bonded, or so
I felt. How could you not be the very first
To bless what I had found? Hence, who else to

Turn to for its salvation? Who better to impress upon
An errant mind it's inexpressible importance,
To convince her of its need for preservation,
Teach of sanctity? I sent you her, my lovely Paige,
So desperately in need of reclamation, to

Be reminded of what she knew so deeply too,
Or had said so, that we were as one being,
A creation not to be betrayed, an act of God.
I forced her there, a sunny flat in San Francisco,
Haven for clear thought, to one who knew.

It seemed a brilliant plan, a dose of solid
Jocelyn. I simply didn't comprehend you'd
Learned by then the folly of Grand Passions
And so were moved to free her, just as
You had been, with virile quick replacement.

Quite amusing, must have been, the liberation of such
A lovely spirit, the loveliest I still have ever known?
The irony as sharp to me as razor to the wrist.
"But didn't you want rid of her?" you asked,
As if sincerely puzzled by my shock.

~

Paige took a deep breath. "Sorry for all the stumbles."

"Don't be silly," Jocelyn answered. "You read perfectly."

"Luke slit his wrists with a razor?" André asked. "Thought he gassed himself in his car."

"Probably just another metaphor," Jocelyn said.

"Or maybe an earlier suicide attempt," Erica added.

"I'm not very metaphorical," André said.

"Actually it's a simile," Paige cut in.

"Metaphor, simile," Erica said. "Who cares? The guy is dead."

"And the saddest part of all," Paige said, "he was survived by not a soul. You're right, Jocelyn, seems like he thought of *us* as his survivors. I feel so bad right now."

"Poor guy," Jocelyn said. She slid around the edge of the Jacuzzi and gave Paige a hug.

"I was so awful to him," Paige said tearfully.

"Hey," Jocelyn said, "water under the bridge. It's okay, hon. It's okay." She held Paige a moment more and edged away. "As his writing tells us, he saw *me* as somewhat responsible. In fact, I *wasn't* puzzled by his shock. Only kind of irritated if I recall. He should have known what would happen if he sent you away like that, Paige. And Frisco was certainly no nunnery."

"I'm lost," Erica said. "What shock? I missed something."

"I know," André said with the pleasure of a kid who has the answer. "He wanted Joss to rehabilitate you, Paige. Something had gone wrong between you and him, and he sent you to Joss to get your head on straight. Right, Joss?"

"Yes," Jocelyn said. "Crazy. Right there in the first line. I was supposed to get her back for him. And you really needed a refuge, right, Paige?"

"I was pretty much lost at that point. No, *really* lost."

"Were you aware, Joss," Erica asked, "that you were supposed to reclaim Paige for him?"

"Actually, I felt more like a dumping ground."

"Had he discussed what the problem was?"

"He phoned me, desperate, said he'd reached the breaking point with Paige, needed relief, couldn't concentrate on his studies, was at his wit's end, they were both suffering horribly, and would I take her off his hands."

"He put it like that?" Paige asked. "Take me off his hands?"

"No," Jocelyn said. "But at that particular time, unbeknownst to Luke, he and I were in different universes. He was just plain mistaken that I knew the sacredness of what he called Grand Passions. Yes, for a while with Tony I believed all the sentimental bullshit. The idea of romantic fulfillment was thrown at us from every media angle in those days – soul mates, eternal love – and I'd fallen for it with Tony until the abortion and his choosing his wife and ministry over me. Then along came André and showed me how easy it was to become un-suicidal."

She turned toward André who was lolling in the warm water, his back toward her.

"Thank you, André," she said, tugging his silver braid. "You see, Paige, I listened to Luke's long distance lamentations that his romance with you had gone bad, and as he described your state I felt more sympathy for you than for him. He was really worried about you, didn't know what to do. I was convinced you needed a refuge, not to be salvaged for him, but to be freed from the burden of the totally mythical Grand Passion. Of course, I didn't tell him that. You both needed to be freed from the pressure of True Love. I knew I couldn't help him restore what he'd lost, but I thought I could help you, Paige, to move on."

"Did you want to go to Joss, Paige?" asked André. "Did you even know her?"

"Luke and I had driven across the country one summer, nineteen sixty-eight, and spent some time with Jocelyn in San Francisco. I really liked her. She showed us the city. It was amazing at that time, hippies everywhere, even the mailmen and cops wore ponytails. You and I got along great, didn't we, Jocelyn?"

"Like you were my soul sister."

"And Luke and I were in our so called Grand Passion on that first trip. It was glorious."

"And I sensed where it was headed," Jocelyn said, "the same place they all end up."

"Heartbreak Hotel," André said. "The end of Lonely Street."

"So you weren't surprised by Luke's call?" Erica asked.

"No. But saddened. Another piece of evidence that it was all a myth."

"But you didn't mention to him that you were no longer in his corner," Erica noted.

"No. I wanted to help Paige. She was in more trouble. I knew Luke would be okay, really miserable, hurt, confused, but he would survive. I wasn't sure about Paige. She became my first priority."

"Why'd you end up going, Paige?" André asked. "Soul sisters?"

With a forefinger Paige twirled a strand of her thick hair. "No, not soul sisters. I didn't want to leave him but he convinced me. He asked me did I love him, and I said yes, and he said, then go because he needed some time to himself, to get his act together. He needed me to get out of my depression. I *was* suicidal. He *was* really worried about me, and had reason to be. He tried everything to bring me out of it – doctors, women's lib groups, and counseling, which carried a stigma in those days. The doctor said I should eat less salt. Therapy had no effect. Luke's usual method was that when I fell into one of my blue funks – we called them my *traumas* – he distracted me by changing the scenery."

"Changing scenery?" Erica asked.

"At first, when my blues weren't so deep, it was something simple, like he'd get me to walk up the street with him to the ice cream store, or go to a movie, drive around, make love, you know, and eat chocolate pudding afterwards. Then he'd say, 'You see? Life isn't so bad, is it?' But the deeper my depression went, the more radical the diversion he came up with, like camping in the woods, heading off to Woodstock, or anything to distract me from my mood. I'm sure that was how he came up with the final idea of my going to Jocelyn in San Francisco."

"One helluva diversion," André said. "And leaving your classes?"

"Yes." Paige's hair twirling had become tugging. "There was nothing I cared about in Columbus. I'd left my husband, given up my dear little Yorkie, my house. My parents were about to banish me because of my deserting the marriage. All I had was Luke, and he wanted to escape from me, even tried to get his own room, but I kept calling him there and telling him I needed him, ended up living *there* with him. I was a total wreck."

"Sure sounds like it," Erica said dismissively.

"Ever feel like that, Erica?" Jocelyn asked.

"No. I always disliked men, just used them. One walked out, another walked in. Don't *need* anyone."

"Like André," Jocelyn said.

"I don't dislike men," he answered, "or use them. Not even attracted to them. Might have had a fantasy or two about Elvis, though."

"But you don't need a *particular* woman," Jocelyn said, ignoring his attempt at levity, "just a generic one as long as you find her appealing. Not searching for a soul mate."

"Okay, maybe I'm like Erica in *that* sense." He stretched his legs out in the water, accidentally brushing against Erica's. "I do the math – one plus one is two, not one. And I'm not analytical about all this stuff, but it seems to me that, at the moment, there's one giant elephant here with us in the gazebo."

Jocelyn smiled. "Care to put a name on that elephant, André?"

"Okay. I understand what cracked up *your* Grand Passion, Joss. Someone in Tony's church ratted him out, that he was seeing some sexy little blond. He was forced to decide between you and his family, wife and three boys, right? And he gave up the Grand Passion for them, right?"

"More or less," Jocelyn said, "if it ever was True Love for him."

"Okay, I get that. So, Paige, according to this letter you just read, Luke sounded head over heels for you, like Joss was for Tony. And apparently you felt the same way, right?"

"I did, yes."

"So here's the name of the elephant: *what went sour, Paige, between you and Luke?*"

Jocelyn felt an inward glow. André had perfectly nailed the whole point of this exploration, one which, long ago when Paige had come to her from Columbus, she'd tried to discover but had eventually given up to focus exclusively on Paige's future not her past. Her past had seemed an irresolvable muddle, as if she had been hiding something, or not able to face it, whatever it was.

During these thoughts, the group had turned their attention to Paige, whose tendency to blush had, it seemed, reached its apex. She burst into tears.

10

With Jocelyn's arms around her, Paige eventually settled down. Dripping wet, André had hustled off and come back with a box of tissues.

"Should've realized we'd need these," he said, slipping into the water.

Jocelyn perspired from the updraft of warmth from the hot tub and from the humidity of the late summer afternoon. Eyes closed, Erica, immersed to her neck in the water, seemed to be in her own world.

Expending a handful of tissues, Paige wiped her cheeks, blew her nose.

"I can't tell you how uncomfortable all this is for me. I've left self-analysis long ago. What I'm into now negates the necessity of this. We rid ourselves of stress through the deep rest in meditation. We understand that in our ignorance we've all made mistakes, in not living in touch with our own Being. We transcend our pasts, purify our nervous systems, without having to go back into the dirt."

"Transcend?" Jocelyn said. "Or maybe hide your head in the sand, in denial."

"Maharishi laughs, well, laughed – he's gone now – at psychoanalysis. I know that's your thing, Jocelyn, so we've taken opposite paths, and I'm not trying to convince you of anything, just that this situation, right here and now, is antithetical to what I believe."

"But you've come all the way here," Erica said, eyes still closed. "Why?"

"Because Jocelyn saved me back then. She *was* a refuge, edged me out of my misery and into living again."

"But not by reconstructing you for Luke."

"No, by *de*constructing me and him. By nudging me into accepting another way of looking at things and making me feel okay with it."

"I pushed her into the city," Jocelyn explained. "Tried to get her to see that she and Luke were finished. That there was no way of repairing what happened. A Grand Passion is like a rare and fragile teacup, filled to the brim with joy, yes, but easily broken, and once broken, impossible to repair. The only thing left, a big, sloppy mess."

"Good metaphor," André said.

"But Joss repaired *you*, at least, right, Paige?" Erica asked, sitting up to her waist in the water and opening her eyes as if returning to the real world.

"Yes, by pushing me to hide my head, not in the sand, but in that wonderful place. Jocelyn had lost Tony, no going back, and had gone to you, André. Like, she knew that the path led forward not back."

"I had no such vision, Paige. I was lost until André suddenly appeared. He was impossible to turn down."

"But now, Paige, you're here with us," Erica said, "aren't you? Even though it goes against your beliefs."

Recovered from the need of tissues, Paige, the box still on her lap, smiled weakly.

"There's karma here. I've known it for a long time. And suddenly it arrived in two phases, first Luke's poem, which hit me like a brick, and then Jocelyn's phone call. I guess this is the third phase right now, this elephant in the gazebo."

"Didn't you just say you *transcend* your past?" Erica asked.

"But one still has to pay one's karmic debts."

"Excuse me?" Erica said.

"The Law of Karma is as immutable as gravity. What we send out not only in this life but past ones, always comes back. But by growing in consciousness in the meantime, we can be strong enough not to be devastated when it finally hits us. Coming here is karmic payback for me, you see?"

"Do you really believe that crap?"

"Yes, Erica, I do."

"So you're as deranged as these rightwing Christians, believing humans lived among dinosaurs, fantasizing about sitting with angels and harps after they kick the bucket? Or of being eternally tortured in fire and brimstone?"

"Easy, Erica," Jocelyn said. "We all need to believe in something. Even a belief in nothing is a belief. We don't need to know why Paige decided to leave her safe cocoon in Iowa, just that she's here with us, among friends. And if we can help her pay her so called karmic debts, we're blessed to do so, aren't we? I'm searching for my own closure, which seems about the same thing."

"I don't feel that kind of need," Erica said. "I'm just here to visit home again, to see old friends, get out of the rain and fog for a while. And I have to tell you that tomorrow I'm having lunch with my daughter and grandkids, and seeing my great-granddaughter in person for the first time."

"Kinda in that category myself," André said. "I mean about seeing old friends, not paying debts."

"Yes," Jocelyn said, "you two weren't as deeply involved with Paige and Luke, don't have nearly as much to resolve."

"But Paige," André said. "You didn't answer my original question. What happened between you and Luke? Must have been something extreme to make you suicidal. To me, you've never seemed anything close to that."

"And I think you know the answer, Paige," Jocelyn added.

"Maybe I do know, but might you give me a break for a while? I need some time."

André smiled. "Change of scenery, eh? Okay, here's a question for you, Joss. I mean, this poem *is* about you, isn't it?"

"What might that question be, André dear?"

"Chicken bones in your bed?"

"Yeah," Erica broke in, "I was wondering about that too."

Jocelyn's turn to blush. "Okay, just that I was a slob, didn't keep house. Like Hillary says, not meant to stay home and bake cupcakes."

"Cookies," Erica objected. "Hillary said *cookies*. But, girl, garbage in your bed?"

"Luke exaggerates. But I spent a lot of time alone when I was seeing Tony. He was busy with his ministry, and when I wasn't at work, I read in bed, watched TV in bed and ate my meals in bed. The only time I cleaned up was when I knew Tony was coming. So, dammit, a chicken bone might have fallen off a plate, unnoticed."

"How did Luke know about the bones?" Erica asked.

"Casual sheets?" André quoted from Luke's poem.

"All right," Jocelyn said, inching away from Paige, "you cornered me. I knew it was coming. Luke was pretty clear."

"Yeah," André said. "The abortion. Never knew about that."

"I slept with Luke only once. I was lonely, nothing better to do, as he says."

"So, the trip to Wilmington," André said. "You must have met me shortly after, according to what Luke wrote. When I saw you downtown."

"Wannamaker's," Erica added. "I didn't know about the abortion either, Joss."

"Luke's kid," André said. "Must have been tough on him. Apparently didn't agree with the idea."

"No, not Luke's. The child was Tony's."

"Tony's?" Erica said. "I'm confused."

"Okay, okay. Listen. I'll tell you. This is *my* karmic debt, Paige. Or my confession. I'm not proud of it. And I've never spoken about any of this until now." She took a deep breath, straightened her back, her feet and ankles still in the water. "I did sleep with Luke, one time, before he moved in with you, Erica. My idea, not his. He used to drive me home to my apartment after Tony's Sunday night services, come in with me. We'd talk, watch the Sunday Night Movie."

"How'd you meet him?" Erica asked. "This is hot news. You slept with him while he was visiting me late at night?"

"I did, Erica. He talked about you a lot, felt conflicted, but as I said, before he moved in with you, before I'd met you. I met him at Tony's church. That was where a bunch of antiwar types, civil rights people, gathered. Luke was one of those. I didn't drive, so he took me home one night, and we grew to be friends. I was alone a lot, as I said, and we discussed things – not only politics but books. I liked to read the classics, and Tony wrote poetry and got me into reading philosophy. Luke and I had nice conversations. I liked him. We joked. Then one night it happened, that's all. I came on to him, kinda had to persuade him. He seemed shocked. 'But you're with Reverend Perrino,' he said. Luke felt outclassed. But I managed to seduce him."

"You *were* a knockout," André said.

"I worked hard at that."

A bright green katydid landed on the plank floor next to the lemonade pitcher, moved its long antennae.

"Didn't use protection?" Erica asked Jocelyn.

"Hmm. Tony didn't like condoms, the pill was too new – my doctor didn't trust it – so we used the rhythm method. I kept track of my periods, knew the safe zones."

"One good thing about old age," André said. "Automatic birth control." He looked for smiles but found none. The katydid whirred up and settled, perfectly camouflaged, on a viburnum leaf next to the railing.

"When it wasn't safe," Jocelyn went on, "Tony and I did other things. The night with Luke was borderline, and later, when I knew

I was pregnant with Tony, then the borderline had been close enough for me to convince Luke he was the one. As I said, I'm not proud of any of this. It's a terrible thing I did. I'd almost tucked it away as forgotten until Luke reminded me of it in his poem. Through the whole ordeal, I always managed to hide my head in the sand about his feelings."

"I don't get it," Erica said. "Why didn't you just tell Tony, if that's whose kid it was?"

"I *did* tell him. I was overjoyed, would have loved to have his child. Then came the first crack in the dream of me and Tony."

"Sounds to me," Erica said, "that the first crack was you having sex with Luke. I mean, if you and Tony were in the middle of True Love."

"Touché, Erica," Jocelyn said. "Luke was a betrayal, you're right."

"If you 'truly' loved Tony," Erica pressed on, "you wouldn't have slept with Luke."

"No, you're wrong there. I truly loved Tony. Like Luke loved Paige but slept with you that Christmas on the acid trip."

"Hey, ladies," André broke in. "Everybody slept with everybody. But Erica has a point, Joss. You and Luke did put a crack in that Grand Passion tea cup you mentioned."

"Except it didn't mean anything with Luke."

"Listen to yourself, Joss," Erica said, scoffing.

Joss held up a finger in the stop pose. "You're right. Right is right. I did put the first crack in Tony and me. I did. Except that..."

Erica rolled her eyes. "You're trying to weasel out of it."

"You're right, Erica. But listen. When I told Tony I was pregnant, Tony didn't know anything about Luke and me. I had no intention of telling Tony about that one slipup. It was meaningless. And there was no doubt the baby was Tony's."

"Meaningless?" Erica said. "To Tony?"

"Well, don't you see? When I told Tony I was pregnant, he immediately, no hesitation, he mentioned an abortion. 'We'll take care of it,' he said, almost like a reflex. I'll never forget those words." She shuddered. "Luke wasn't part of the issue at all. That showed me where I stood."

"This is getting complicated," André said. "Then how did Luke get into the conversation?"

"Wow!" Jocelyn answered, straightening up again, her back throbbing. "I guess my karma is hitting me full in the face at this moment."

"Okay," Paige said. "Please stop making fun of me."

"Come on, Joss," André coaxed. "Let it out. It's what this gathering is all about, isn't it?"

"Tony didn't want the baby," Erica explained, "and didn't know about Joss's *meaningless* thing with Luke."

Jocelyn took a deep breath. She rubbed her lower lumbar.

"Tony didn't want the baby," she carried on, frowning. "He wanted me to get rid of it, and his response was immediate – 'We'll take care of it.' I was crushed. We argued for days, and after all his explanations, I finally submitted. But he didn't have time from the church to deal with all the details, didn't know how to go about it and talked me into doing the research and making the arrangements. He'd support me, pay for everything, but it had to be hush hush. I was devastated, but I agreed though I didn't have a clue where to start."

"Illegal as hell back then," Erica said. "I didn't feel it was an option when I got pregnant with Lori."

"My doctor cringed when I asked him," Jocelyn went on. "Mum on the subject. But Luke had a friend in medical school, his college roommate. So I got the horribly devious idea of telling Luke the child was his. But that forced me to tell Tony about my one night stand."

"How'd he react to that little factoid?" Erica asked.

"He took it right in stride, as if he was liberal minded about infidelity. The pregnancy put more on his mind than such a minor offense as a one night stand. After all, he'd still been sleeping with his wife."

"Jesus," Erica said, "what is this, Days of Our Lives?"

"This is nothing to joke about," Paige said.

Erica glared at her across the hot tub.

"Yes," Jocelyn went on, "my night with Luke hardly phased Tony. I guess I was using Luke to try to make Tony jealous, but he saw Luke as small fry, yet, suddenly useful."

"A true man of the Lord," Erica said. "It's why I hate religion."

A wasp flew in, upward, finding its mud nest at the apex of the roof. Paige looked at it fearfully.

"Don't worry, Paige," André said. "They don't care about us."

"And I agreed to the plan," Jocelyn continued, "but there was a problem with Tony's paying the two hundred dollars. How would he explain that to Luke? He didn't want Luke to have to bear the expense. That was a lot in those days. So he dealt with it by saying he realized that Luke didn't earn very much and, after all, he – Tony, that is – had left me alone too much so was responsible in a way, and would pay half."

"And Luke fell for it," Erica said. "Not surprising. But devious as hell, like you say, for a preacher and for you, Joss, Luke's supposed friend."

"Yes. I was desperate. And it was unforgivable. But I convinced Luke. He asked me if I'd been seeing a third guy, forced me to show him the dates to prove Tony had been out of town."

"Even said he'd marry you?" Erica asked.

"Or that his parents would adopt. The issue eventually shifted from whose child it was to the morality of abortion in general. Luke thought it would be murder, said it was more than just a collection of cells, begged to take the child himself. We met with Tony, and Tony finally convinced him otherwise. Said the ultimate decision was in my hands. Luke was greatly enamored of Tony, respected his moral viewpoint – the whole abortion debate as we now know it. Tony insisted it was my choice, my body. And I insisted too, so Luke finally realized his only options were to wash his hands of the whole thing or help me do what I was determined to do. He submitted to the plan. His medical school friend found out about someone in Wilmington, and we did it."

"According to Luke's letter," André said, "that was about the time I picked you up in Wannamaker's."

"Yes. As I was recovering, the church board somehow found out about Tony and me – the final crack. He had to choose, and did, and left for Buffalo. I was shattered, recovered from the operation, and was magically diverted into raw pleasure by this flashy, engaging fellow at the perfume counter asking me which male cologne women like best."

She smiled at André. He flicked some water toward her, which she dodged.

"Which cologne women like best?" Erica said. "A pretty good pickup line."

Silence followed Jocelyn's tale except for a pair of cardinals chirruping to each other in the maple branches.

The longtime friends sipped their iced teas, didn't meet one another's eyes.

"My being with André," Jocelyn continued, "freed Luke up to become more serious with you, Erica. He'd been hanging around, taking care of me, nothing sexual. Tony had asked him to watch over me, but Luke would have done it anyway."

"He didn't say a thing to me about all this," Erica said. "Just that you were his friend and we should hang out with you and André."

"I didn't know either," André said. "Just that you were the hottest number in Lancaster."

"Did you and Tony keep in touch?" Paige asked.

"An occasional letter. He transferred eventually to a church in Santa Barbara, then was defrocked for seducing women he was counseling. I wasn't surprised. As much as I idealized him, he was just a lowlife lecher, that's all. And I was his victim, one of his many easy pickings. Somehow André gets away with it. But it certainly didn't work for Tony. I guess artists are granted more leeway than pastors." She sneered, kicked some water toward André. "Men – bleached blond hair and a miniskirt does it every time – Bill Clinton, every damn one."

"Monica was no bleached blond," André noted.

"Yeah," Erica said, "how *do* you get away with it, André? Even with all your women, I've never thought of you as a letch."

"Get away with what?"

"No bitterness from your exes, no moral condemnation because of your lifestyle. We just accept your hedonism, dig it, actually."

"Because he's not to blame," Jocelyn said. "It's his nature, beyond judgment. Do we condemn a horny lynx? And if we embrace the obvious, it's only ourselves to blame. For me, I decided to go for it about two minutes after we started sniffing sample fragrances from each other's wrists."

"Back to the elephant," André said, waving a hand against the derisive compliments. "There's a line here in the poem – let me find it. Here it is: 'virile quick replacement.' Anyone care to comment?"

"I will," Jocelyn responded. "That was you for me, André. It was Jesse for you, right, Paige?"

Would her blushing ever stop? "Yes, that's right," she answered, head hung.

"Jesse?" Erica said. "Who the hell is Jesse?"

"A surfer guy I knew," Paige answered. "I met him at a hippie hangout on the beach – the Family Dog. There was a guru type leader, Steve something."

"Gaskin," Jocelyn said.

"Gaskin, that's right. And all the flowerchildren gathered together Sunday nights, got high and listened to his sermons."

"Like Ken Kesey?" André asked. "And the Merry Pranksters?"

"Right," Jocelyn said, "without the psychedelic school bus. That place was wild and wooly. Right out of *Hair*. Paige was writing desperate letters to Luke, begging him to let her come back, and he was answering that he still needed time. It became more and more obvious to me that he was done with Paige. So I called Jesse, had him drop by the Family Dog, dragged Paige there, and found an excuse to leave the two of them alone. Then things took their natural course."

"You persuaded me," Paige interrupted. "Until this moment, I never knew you set that up."

"Yes. You needed an André. Jesse was perfect. You admitted he turned you on, no sin in that. He was a hunk."

"You kept telling me, 'go for it, do it, do it.' You said, 'Luke's finished with you. Get on with your life.'"

"You didn't seem to mind the results."

"No. You're right. Before Jesse, not once had I been able to stop thinking about Luke. Finally giving in to the present was a huge relief."

"It says here '*quick* replacement,'" André said. "How long between Tony and me, Joss?"

"A month. And, like me, soon instead of sobbing endlessly, Paige was beaming, hitting the beaches, learning to hang ten, smoking hash from a hookah. Suicide problem solved."

"And were you amused, Joss," Erica asked, "as Luke claims, by setting that up?"

"I wouldn't say *amused*. That's Luke's sarcasm. But it's always satisfying to make a positive difference. Shortly after that, I applied to Cal-Berk in psych. Paige's liberation had whetted my appetite for a career."

11

Wasps coming and going above, the gazebo session neared its end with a humorous reminiscence of André's old place as described in Luke's writing. The small, two story, white block building on the then edge of the city's ghetto was dubbed the Candy Factory because its original use had been the manufacturing of lollipops. André took it over as combination living quarters and studio, the faint aroma of sugar and paint thinner ever present. They also talked of Luke's description of their nineteen sixty-seven summer.

"When Luke and I first started talking in Columbus that October," Paige said, "he spoke so fondly of those months with the three of you."

"Anyway," Jocelyn ended the exchange, "there weren't *that* many chicken bones on my bed."

Before they broke for an afternoon respite, they discussed dinner plans. After a number of options, they chose the traditional Stockyard Inn, next to the still functioning meat processing facility on the city's north side.

"I was a waitress at the Inn," Paige said, "when I lived here with Luke, then André. I know it's a meat place, but I'd like to go back. Fond memories, actually. And I'm sure there's something on the menu I can deal with."

"What about the smell of all that beef?" Erica asked.

"I'll make do. Please don't concern yourselves. I'd like to go there, really."

In her own room Jocelyn undressed, pulled the fentanyl patch from the small of her back to be replaced after her bath, good for another three days. She wished it worked better. After turning on the water for the tub, she looked closely in the mirror, felt for any signs of swollen lymph nodes on her neck or under her arms. She cringed at the minutely creeping jaundice in her complexion. Back home her oncologist was deciding on the treatment protocol for the tumor on her pancreas. Regardless, Jocelyn had enough time to settle her affairs, Luke's implications of decades old blame among them.

She sank into the deep tub, inhaling the fragrance of bath oil André had placed in a cabinet for guests. Yes, she had acted in *Paige's* interests not Luke's. Since receiving his deathbed letter she'd been feeling deep guilt about that choice. The gazebo session had eased the feeling a bit. Way back then, her once semireligious conviction in Grand Passions had been replaced by a more realistic view of love, but apparently Luke had never outgrown his belief in picket fences. She should have talked to him about her betrayal at some point, but she'd thought he would let the matter go. Paths cross, after all, a natural part of living.

Much more profound, however, was her guilt for having allowed Luke a lifetime of believing he'd aided in the death of his own unborn child. He'd said, back then, that it felt like murder. He didn't believe in abortion, but Tony had convinced him that the woman's choice trumped the man's. The argument hadn't been an easy one, but Luke had finally relented.

She'd several times later wanted to tell him he'd been manipulated, to beg his forgiveness, but now — too late. How she wished Luke were here to participate in these discussions! She longed to set things straight, give him a hug and say how sorry she was. It was unforgivable.

Her job now was to forgive herself. She was sure Luke had led a decent and productive life. Certainly, she, herself, in spite of that one dreadful error, had done so, of that she was quite satisfied. Not that she wouldn't have had the abortion, but she shouldn't have lied about Luke's having been the father. That was sinful.

Paige, however, presented another side of things – the elephant in the gazebo. Jocelyn smiled at André's clumsy attempt at metaphor. If she'd thought Paige would fess up, she'd been sadly mistaken. But sometime this weekend, Paige would have to come clean – if she didn't owe it to Jocelyn for having kept her in the dark, she owed it to her own karmic forces. Jocelyn deeply believed in the cleansing value of confession. And she knew Paige had something to confess about what happened between her and Luke. Having the *blues* simply didn't suffice.

~

After their rest Erica drove the quartet to the Inn, the local nickname of the time proven eatery, where André had reserved a table.

As they eagerly began their first round of food in the crowded, historic hotel with white tablecloths and white linen napkins, Paige remembered working as a cocktail waitress in the bar, amid cigar smoke, masculine laughter, country music, large gratuities, and many, many invitations for extracurricular activities, several of which she'd accepted. She'd guiltlessly saved the proceeds from these "dates" for a trip to Italy to enroll in a teacher training course for meditation. The Inn brought back the pleasures and the turmoil of her year in this lovely but dull city.

All but Paige had several rounds of cocktails, she a glass of cranberry juice.

When a group entered wearing breathing masks, Erica, holding a tenderloin tip on her fork, wondered aloud how they intended to eat.

"Why wear surgical masks to go out to a crowded restaurant?" she said.

"Probably just making a statement," Jocelyn surmised, dipping a small piece of crab cake into spicy rémoulade sauce.

The conversation turned to the Ebola epidemic in the news and then on to the upcoming danger of running out of antibiotics altogether, any infection even the common cold leading to certain death.

"They'll find an answer," André said with his usual optimism. He sliced into his blood rare filet mignon, "just like they did with AIDS."

"They haven't found a cure," Jocelyn objected, "only a very complicated and expensive treatment protocol."

"Anyway," he added, "the masks add some mystery. But they could design them more fashionably, like veils, maybe. With an opening for food. I might work on that." He smiled. "But as for making a statement, that new group in Iraq couldn't have done better than with Jihadi John, all in black and holding that scimitar. Pure genius as a symbol for terror."

In shock, Paige glanced up from her poached pear and goat cheese salad.

"I'm just saying," André explained, "from a purely design point of view." He speared another piece of his steak.

~

Later, back at André's, all but Paige agreed that they were too tipsy for serious discussion, so they changed clothes and gathered in a rec room in the basement where André had set up a man cave with leather furniture, a juke box with all the classic hits from the sixties and seventies, a pool table, a dartboard and a small bar. At one end of the large room sat a treadmill, a workout bike, a rowing machine, and a rack of shiny weights. Ornately framed old posters

of horror films adorned the walls, prominent among them the Creature of the Black Lagoon. They were presented as if they'd been
done by the Dutch Masters.

Paige sank back in a soft chair and watched the others boogie
until André yanked her into the middle of things. They did a mini
version of a dance called "The Stroll." They added the Twist, the
Frugue, the Boogaloo, the Mashed Potato, and the Funky Chicken.
They were far from the rock & roll grace of the American Band-
stand of their youth. But aside from occasional bones creaking, they
howled with laughter at each other's moves. Paige was buzzed
enough on the vibes themselves to do a demonstration of her favorite dance from those days, the Pony. She romped comically
around the room in her kurta, tights and stockinged feet, her thick,
wavy, pinned up hair coming undone. She almost forgot about what
would be dominating next morning's discussion session – Luke's
piece to her.

Several times during the carousing, André brushed against her,
touching her fleetingly. Or was it accidental? Either way, those
touches ignited feelings she couldn't ignore. The sensations dis-
turbed her. In the past when such tinglings occurred, she'd done
something about them, one way or another, but it had been nearly
a year since she and William had... And now, here were André, and
Jocelyn, once believers of following one's impulses, and Erica
who'd been simply unphilosophically loose.

Moving close to Paige, André, his pleasing timber scented cologne evident, left his momentary nudges like hidden invitations.
They ignited sparks from sleeping embers, hardly what she needed
at this point in her existence. She should have listened to William
about this trip. Now, suddenly, unexpectedly – the tantalizing old
turmoil.

When she announced her need for sleep, the others stopped
dancing and bid her good night.

"Should I walk you upstairs?" André asked.

"No need." She imitated a drill sergeant saluting. "As you
were, soldiers."

Carrying her beaded slippers, she climbed the long spiral stairs
in the dim light, the music going on from below. She was perspiring
as she opened the door to the small guest apartment and turned on
the light. About to lock the door, her fingers paused on the latch.
Puzzled at herself, she left it open. After all, she reasoned, this isn't

a hotel. On the coffee table next to her yoga mat on the floor sat a small portrait of Guru Dev, Maharishi's master, brought along to keep her in constant touch with the Holy Tradition. In the shower she lathered her body with the Ayurvedic soap she'd brought along. Yes, she was in a state. It had arisen from memories she thought she'd finally, along with aging, managed to get under control.

Sometime later during a restless sleep, she heard a tap on her door. She lay still as stone. She heard the door creak open, the latch closing. She sensed him moving across the room, felt the bed almost unperceptively sag as he sat beside her. Again, his scent. He lay down, edged against her, touched her hip outside her pajamas, drew her against him. And there she was again, the days and nights they'd spent together in that odd candy scented garret, the wonderful wildness, no restrictions.

The first time for her came quickly. Others followed. When she woke with the bright light of morning, he was gone. Had it been a dream? Oh, how she hoped so! But her sleepwear lay heaped on the carpet.

She glanced at the nightstand clock – 10:17, already late for the proposed morning session. Her meditation routine would take an hour. Cutting the time in half would still set the schedule back significantly for the others. She wished she could skip this meeting. But she would certainly need a meditation to fortify herself. She rose, sensed André's smell on her skin, his touches on her breasts, his taste on her lips.

~

"What happened to Paige?" Erica asked, munching a piece of seven grain toast covered with grape jam.

Caroline set a stack of pancakes on the table.

"Probably worn out from doing the Pony," André offered, grabbing a few flapjacks and dousing them with maple syrup. "Eat up," he said to Jocelyn. "What happened to your appetite? You used to eat like a hound."

"That's not a very nice thing to say to a woman," she answered, smiling. "I've managed to master my appetite. After a lifetime struggle, I might add. I deserve respect, not ridicule." She winked.

"Paige is meditating, no doubt," Erica said, rolling her eyes and pouring cream on fresh strawberries. "And we're postponing her poem, right? Since I'm headed out to meet my offspring, which should be a drag for all involved."

"*Offspring?* Weird way of putting it," André said, devouring his food.

"Well, my relationship with them is distant and crappy. But I can't get out of this reunion."

"Don't you have any feelings for them?" Jocelyn asked, finished with her half eaten croissant but sipping Caroline's delicious almond flavored coffee.

"It's not *my* feelings, but theirs. Lori has never forgiven me though my aunt gave her everything I couldn't, including college and, hell, a normal life. We've never made any secret of what happened, so my biological motherhood can't be denied. We honor it on the edges of our lives."

"So," Jocelyn said to André, "why don't you and I retrace our old steps around town. The memories will be pleasant. Erica doesn't care if we take a walk without her, do you, dear?"

"No, but I wouldn't mind a little tubing on the river. Maybe tomorrow?"

"Paige is in Nirvana at the moment," Jocelyn added, "and won't miss us."

"We can't just leave without letting her know," André said.

"Slip a note under her door. Tell her we'll be back for lunch. We'll get to Luke's poem to her this afternoon."

After breakfast André did as instructed about the note; Erica took off for Manheim, the once quiet village now a part of urban sprawl; and André and Jocelyn strolled arm in arm toward the city square – James Street west to Queen, south toward the main intersection with King. The streets were crowded with the Labor Day traffic, many tourists browsing the shops. The couple passed the bustling Central Market.

"When did they move this place from the South Side?" Jocelyn asked.

"Years now. Part of the whole redevelopment plan, fresh vegetables and sausage center stage. Lancaster as the Horn of Plenty. The architecture sucks, but the firm was cheap. It's nice walking with you, Joss."

"And the Brunswick Hotel transformed into Hotel Lancaster. *Tres* posh. I thought the Brunswick would be a historic landmark by now. And Zimmerman's Diner – Yorgo's?"

"Greek."

"No more chicken corn soup for lunch?"

"The gyros aren't bad, though."

The former five & tens had become art galleries, antique shops, fashion boutiques, all the once familiar places gone.

"This is really touristy," Jocelyn lamented as they approached the city square. "Oh, and Wannamaker's now a Marriot."

"Yeah, but there's a plaque. Says, 'first meeting place of Dr. Jocelyn Consolo and renowned artiste André Roulier.'"

She edged against him. "There *should* be a plaque, shouldn't there?"

He took her hand. "Come on, I want to show you something."

In the heat and humidity of the summer day, he led her a block eastward past the court house on King, to Duke, then a block south to Water Street.

"My God!" she said, stopping. "The Candy Factory!"

André beamed.

"A gallery!" She smiled at him. "Makes perfect sense."

"For new artists. Come on, it's open."

Inside through the polished oak doorway with André's name over it in gilded lettering, they were greeted by a young woman of Asian descent.

"Daddy! Good morning!"

"Joss, meet Kiko."

Astonishment growing, Jocelyn reached out and shook hands with a willowy young woman with straight, waist long black hair. Tattoos covered both arms.

"Some of her work is upstairs," André said. He held out his left arm. "She did my tattoo."

A few guests were musing at paintings and sculptures as he led Joss up the open, tightly spiraled steps.

"We used to climb a ladder to get up here," Jocelyn said, coming to grips with this brand new information about her old friend.

"I wanted to keep it that way, but my Board outvoted me. Also, safety regulations."

"Well, yes, its rustic mystique was charming for me the first time, maybe, but a real nuisance with the bathroom downstairs."

As they looked at Kiko's swirling abstractions, Jocelyn added, "So, who is this lovely young woman's mom, if I may ask."

"Her name is Hanako – Hana – came to Armstrong for training to take over as design director in our Tokyo branch. Kiko was born here, bingo, instant citizenship. Who knows, the Republicans might take it away from her. She goes back and forth as her whim dictates. Graduated from Pratt, like me."

"Well, this place is magnificent. You'd never know the grunge it used to be. Bravo, André!"

Back downstairs after Jocelyn's gushing compliments to Kiko about her work and still shaking her head at these revelations, she strolled with André back the way they'd come. They talked about Kiko's upbringing and her preferring to have her own digs downtown rather than a room in the big house.

"A free spirit," André said, "like her mother."

"More so than her dad? I doubt that."

They crossed Queen Street and passed the Chase Bank.

"I'm surprised," Jocelyn said, "you never moved to somewhere more urbane."

"When retirement from Armstrong was coming up, I thought about Cape May, not urbane but picturesque as hell. Then I bought the Weaver Mansion – too cheap to resist. I'm here to stay."

They circled the Civil War monument in the center of the square. Holding her hand, André led her back northward on the west side of Queen, left on Orange to an alleyway toward the building that once held the offices of the local newspapers – the morning *Intelligencer Journal* and the evening *New Era*.

"There used to be a book store here," Jocelyn said. "It's where I met Tony – no plaque."

"Thought you met him in church."

"Me in church? Not before him. No, he picked me up, just like you did."

"Oh. Bookshelves instead of a perfume counter. Makes sense."

"Records, actually. Classical. We both liked Vivaldi. I didn't know Tony was a minister until after the first time we slept together at my place."

"Roll over any chicken bones?"

She punched him. "Be quiet. Luke exaggerated that."

Down the alley they found a nook-like café with outdoor tables and a small fountain. They sat in the shade of mimosa trees, ordered iced *lattes*, an almond cookie for André.

"How do you think all this is going, André?"

"Great. I like sitting here with you. You're a splendid woman, Joss."

"Thanks, but I meant our all being together again, our talks about Luke."

"Oh, sure, whatever. But..."

Jocelyn waited, then with nothing more forthcoming she said, "That's it? *Whatever?* You were about to say something more."

"But hardly for me to judge."

"Out with it, you old fox."

"All right. Did you really leave Luke thinking he contributed to the death of his unborn child?"

"Oh." Her neck suddenly warmed. "I thought no one had picked up on that."

Sparrows chattered in the branches.

"Pretty obvious, Joss, and a bit of a shock. Doesn't seem like something you would do."

"It was me, all right – but under the influence of the Grand Passion. Not that I don't take full blame. You're right, André, but perhaps youth could excuse it at the time, even though as all these years went on, there was plenty of opportunity for me to tell him. Inexcusable."

"He might have felt a little better."

A sparrow with a tiny black bib alighted on the edge of the table, checked things out and darted away. Jocelyn smiled.

"Then again," André went on, "*I* might have filled him in too, about my being with Paige. Not that I felt guilty, actually, but at least we could have talked it through."

"Hardly comparable to what I did. What can I say except we all make mistakes, sometimes horrible ones. Not being honest with Luke was the worst thing I've ever done. But at least I got us all back together here and confessed. That's something, isn't it, dear André? Can *you* forgive me, at least?"

"Do you even need to ask?"

"Well, it would feel so good to hear the words."

"I'm as far away from a priest as any man can be."

"That is undoubtedly true. But it wasn't as a priest I meant, just hearing it from a friend."

André looked at her, reached across the table for her hand, held it softly. "Joss, sweetheart, I forgive you. You're an exquisite woman, and whatever mistakes you've made, Luke included, I have no doubt you've made up for them and more. I mean it, truly."

Jocelyn felt the tears coming, grabbed a napkin.

"Now," André said. "Say five Hail Mary's, and sin no more."

She had to smile as she blew her nose.

"Anyway, Joss, all this meeting stuff is for you, right?"

"What do you mean?"

"You're the one who thinks Luke's poems are important some-how. The rest of us are kinda embarrassed, exposed. We're doing it for you, out of respect. It's your gig, baby doll."

The young waitress set down their *lattes* and his cookie. They sipped.

"I got us together for Luke."

"Luke made his point in his letters, don't you think?" He seemed to be waiting, then said, "Are you okay, Joss?"

"Yes. Glad to be getting these feelings out."

"No. Are you o-kay?"

"What do you mean?"

"Jesus. I mean, are you well?"

"What makes you think I'm not, André?"

"I know you, Joss. You're not the usual dynamo. Not even close."

"I'm seventy-two for God's sake."

"Okay. Then we'll leave it at that."

"Just because I haven't yanked you into bed."

"Yeah, that's what's been worrying me."

"You jerk. You're still incapable of being serious."

"You're wrong. I'm deeply serious about keeping things light."

They smiled, sipped in silence, in the background only muted voices, distant street sounds and the plash of the fountain. The sparrow showed up again, lingered and fluttered off.

"It's incredible," Jocelyn said. "You slept with all three of us."

He adjusted his napkin nervously.

"André, I'd be really interested in..."

He aligned the salt and pepper shakers.

"Well, in your critical comparison."

He scratched his beard, then tossed some cookie crumbs onto the slate walkway. Instantly, the sparrows arrived in a small flock.

"I don't think I've ever seen you embarrassed before, André."

He coughed. "Never been asked for a comparison-contrast essay on this particular subject."

"But since it's my *gig* this weekend, would you mind?"

"Uh, what was the question again?"

"You're well aware of the question."

"Okay. Well, hmm, every woman is unique. Like, uh, every work of art. Like every snowflake. Hey, how do they really know that about snowflakes, anyway?"

She scoffed. "Of course, but works of art, as you kindly objectify us, can be described, can they not?"

"By art historians, maybe, and dealers for sure, but not by other artists. To most of us all others' work is shit."

She smiled. "All right, André. This is the one aspect of your character that always maddened me. You never say what you think."

He smiled back. "That's because, sweetheart, I carefully avoid the pitfalls involved in thinking."

After André paid the check, he suggested they walk back by Musser Park. With traffic backed up along the way on East Orange, they passed the still functioning nightclub, The Village, the door padlocked at the early hour.

"Remember Daisy Mae, the go-go queen?" André asked.

"Gross and sweaty," Jocelyn answered. "You could whiff her makeup the second you entered the place."

"Randy photographed her, you know. Along with you and Erica."

"Don't remind me of that. God! The college actually closed the exhibit because of my prints. I hope Randy burned them."

"The media debate over free expression made you famous around here. He probably got them out every once in a while and...."

"Don't say that."

"You were a voluptuous beauty, right out of Renoir."

"Just be quiet. I wasn't fat."

"No, I didn't mean that."

Half a block across Duke, he pointed out the building where Erica and Luke once shared an apartment in back.

"I recall our crazy card games," Jocelyn said, "stoned out of our gourds, couldn't remember the bids or what was trump."

"Hardly mattered. Good times, Joss."

"And those plays we tried to read. I'll never forget you trying to read Iago. We were atrocious."

"Except for Erica," André said. "She was a star. Should have got serious about acting."

When they crossed to the small park on Walnut Street, the heat and humidity increasing, they found an empty bench in the shade of chestnut trees, the scent of newly cut grass.

"Lovely," she said. "I used to imagine Tony and me living over in one of those condos. They were brand new back then, those trees just saplings."

"No climbing down a ladder to use the toilet?"

She gripped his knee. "Your renovation is spectacular. Luke really admired and respected you, André."

"Yeah, I liked him too. Very enthusiastic dude." The odor of barbeque wafted by on the warm breeze.

"He told me you were a role model," she said. "That he stole part of your identity for himself."

"Luke didn't need a role model."

"He said he'd always lacked confidence until that summer, that we changed him, helped him grow, said by the time he hit Ohio State he was walking tall for the first time. I..."

André looked at her. "You're crying again, Joss."

She wiped her tears with a thumb.

"Until today, I've never seen you cry. Not even over Tony, as much as you were hurting."

"Sorry. I'm okay." She found a packet of tissues in her purse, dabbed her cheeks. "Sorry."

He put his arm around her, pulled her close.

"You're the dearest man I've ever known, André."

"It's all right, hon."

"And Luke was dear, too."

"Sure, and you too. And Paige, and Erica."

A Frisbee skidded on the path and stopped at their feet. André bent down, picked it up, flung it back to some kids playing in the grassy field.

"Luke described Erica just right," Jocelyn said. "How she ran, like a gazelle."

"Yes, she was something, all right. Still is. What's wrong, Joss. All weepy, hardly eating. Wincing every time you get up. Tell me."

"Old fucking age," she answered, blowing her nose, "that's all."

12

When Paige came out of the shower and into her small living room, she saw a piece of paper that had been slipped under the door, a note in André's smooth penmanship saying they'd all gone out and would be back for lunch. That would give her time to do her entire programme – pranayama, asanas, meditation and special techniques – one hour.

After she finished, she pulled on loose slacks and a tee shirt and went down to the kitchen where Caroline, in a colorful long skirt, bright red blouse and matching bandana, was swaying her hips to calypso music as she chopped a bunch of kale on a cutting board.

"Good morning, Caroline."

Caroline turned and flashed a gap toothed grin. Large hoop earrings glinted against her dark skin.

"Mornin', Miss Paige. M'just now cookin' up some lunch. You missed breakfast, must be starvin'."

"I'll help myself to some juice. Save a good appetite for the meal you're preparing."

"All right, dearie, m'just get back t'work. Do you mind d'tunes?"

"No, it's happy music. I love the steel drums."

On the counter beside the chopping board sat a cup of chickpeas, a sweet potato, an onion and two bell peppers, yellow and red.

"What are you making, Caroline?"

"Oh, some coconut curry, nice 'n hearty to hold you all through d'afternoon. M'check up on Ayurvedic recipes on d'Internet."

"Might I give you a hand?"

"Why, most certainly. You can wash dese greens while m' chop up d'onion and yam, 'n when m'start 'em brownin', you can cut d'peppehs. Don't be too fussy, just bitesize chunks do d'trick."

Paige smiled, put down her orange juice and took the chopping knife.

With the aroma of the onion rising, Caroline said, "M'always pause befoh m'chop, say a little prayeh. Vegetables real beauties, dey ah, m'muses f'd'day. Den m'saw dat Ayurvedic chefs do d'same ting."

"Yes, true, Caroline. What prayer do you say?"

"Oh, no special words. Just simply admireh d'beauty, 'ave a spot of silence."

"Yes, that's right." Paige did so then began chopping.

Caroline poured broth into a pot.

"M'use veggie broth in honor of your diet, Miss Paige. Mix wit coconut milk, y' see?"

"Sounds delicious. And what spices are those?"

"Oh, dem m'special curry mix – curry powdeh, cayenne peppeh, cinnamon, nutmeg – nutmeg come from Grenadah, dey big on nutmeg, y'know, d'whole island smell like spice – 'n salt, a'course. Den y'need some protein, can use fluffy brown rice orh maybe flatbread. M'go t'Tradeh Joe's dis mornin', pick up some *tandoori naan*. Tradeh Joe, 'im m'sous chef."

"Do you mind if I write down this recipe?"

"Not a'tal, darlin'. Don't 'ave m'name on it. Take it home. Enjoy. M'heat it all up when d'others arrive soon. Now m'mix Ayurvedic beverage m'learn online – coconut wateh wit lime, cardamom, gingeh 'n raw sugah. M'chill it f'lunch."

"Sounds delicious, Caroline. Thank you for being so considerate."

"Mr. André, 'im tell me straight out – make sure t' make Miss Paige 'appy. You get up late dis mornin', 'ad extra-long rest."

"Yes, we danced downstairs last night. Must be getting old. Thank you so much for sharing. I look forward to our lunch."

"Yes'm. Misteh André, 'im never seem t'tireh. M'watch 'im out dere in d'garden chippin' 'way on dem stones, houh afteh houh, all d'day long."

"How long have you worked for him, Caroline?"

"Goin' on nine yeah, now. Me and m'daughteh Crystal cook 'n clean d'place. Crystal, she model for Misteh André sometime. Right now, she take a trip back 'ome, Barbados."

"And André mentioned a woman who lives here – Muriel?"

"Ah, yes. When she 'ear tree ladies come to visit, she take off quick-like f'Maine. You gals scare 'er right off."

"And, uh, how old is she, if I may ask?"

"Oh, not rightly sure. In 'er forties, m' would say. Her in real estate, sell Mr. André dis very 'ouse den move in wit 'im. Clever lady, dat Muriel."

~

Erica had called to alert the group that she'd be late for lunch, to go ahead without her, and when she arrived, the others at the

kitchen table, she said she wasn't hungry and hurried upstairs. Jocelyn put down her spoon, wiped her lips on a napkin and excused
herself. At Erica's door, she knocked lightly.

"Erica, it's me."

"Door's open."

Joss found her friend lying face down on the bed. "What's
wrong, dear?"

"Nothing, I'll be okay. Just need a minute."

"What happened with your family?"

"Same old, same old. Held little Taylor."

Jocelyn sat on the edge of the bed, rubbed Erica's back. "Your
great granddaughter. How old?"

Facing away, Erica said. "Four months. I couldn't have done it
differently, Joss. No way could I have raised Lori on my own."

"So then, you did well. The best things we do are seldom easy,
often filled with regrets."

"I'm just an outsider to them, what can I say, but..."

After a while Jocelyn said, "You're missing an outta sight curry.
Why don't you come down and join us? When you're ready."

"Give me a few minutes, okay?"

"We can talk if you like, just you and me."

"Not now, Joss. I'll come down soon."

~

At Jocelyn's strong request, they held their afternoon session
in the living room alcove. She wanted as few distractions as possible. André wisely placed a box of tissues on both ends of the coffee
table, beside the bowls of fruit chunks and a pitcher of iced pome-
granate tea provided by Caroline. They all opened their papers.

"I feel like I'm handcuffed on the gallows," Paige said, hardly
exaggerating.

"This poem is in numbered parts," Jocelyn said before reading.

Futile Fragments
From Luke Shields to Paige Flanagan Owens
Upon my parting
i
I came across a book of yours today,
An item, when you went away,
Got mixed with mine – poems by
Wallace Stevens for a course we took.

FIVE PATHS CROSSING

I held it as I would a relic,
Felt the stir of past epiphany:
I must read a poem to you, you said,
And turned to "Sunday Morning."

We were new to one another, and I listened
As you read with reverence and suddenly
Were moved to press the pages to
Your lips, a kind of kiss that left

An imprint of your lipstick on
The precious lines. To cherish words
Like that, to feel compelled to share
Your joy with me... You were like no one,

No one, I had ever known before.
I held the book, that moment come
Alive again, then opened it.
On the page a faded scarlet touched

The consummation of the swallow's wings.

ii
Sitting on the floor beside
The shelves, a past renewed, I
Turned the pages, one by one, on which
Your little jotted notes revealed

You listened to your teacher well:
Lush, exotic next to one line there,
Imaginative order here, *abandonment
And legacy, rock as symbol of the earth.*

I turned the pages, when suddenly I
Came across ... my name. Solitary in
The margin, purple ink in your small
Penmanship, it stood a tiny banner

To the line: *Being here together
Is enough.* I'd never seen it there
Before, although such private scribbles
Marked our feeling, its gentle fondness

And its depth. *We make a dwelling in*

Jon Michael Miller

The evening air. For so we had, as swallows
Dipped above us, acrobats of flight,
Wholly for our pleasure, our hearts' song.

iii

My vision blurred, I leafed the pages
Idly then, having found my name
Beside a long forgotten line. Eventually
I went upstairs, fumbled through old souvenirs

And finally found a battered cedar box,
Its hinges dulled with rust. Inside,
Tinted green by time, five photographs
That held the journey of our love.

The first shows you completely nude,
A beach near Monterey, in front of fuming
Surf, your arms stretched out in freedom,
Joyous grin, your swimsuit at your feet.

Next, a roadside under a Wyoming sky,
Breakfast by the van, my sweater
Much too big for you. Tugging your boots on,
You're looking up at me annoyed.

Back home then in Ohio. We studied on a
Blanket by the river, your hair disheveled,
Ringed by glints of sun, your smile as bright
As light that danced upon the water.

Another of you sitting on a picnic table,
Leaning back, the straps of your bikini top
Loose on your brown arms, breasts almost
Revealed, a quiet longing in your eyes.

And on the day you left for good, in your tan
Coat, your arm around a snowman. You'd wrapped
My scarf around its neck and smiled to make me happy
In our time of trial, your cheek against its shoulder.

iv

That day was brittle, clear as loss.
The roads were icy, the airport empty
But for the few other boarders

FIVE PATHS CROSSING

Of your flight. We hardly spoke.

We held each other close, sensed
The import of our act, watched
The workmen roam about the plane,
And when the time had come, you could

Not go. I had to force you out the door.
When you ran back to me, I had to break
Your desperate hug. Incredible how hard
We push for what we deem correct.

But did you ever come to comprehend
I'd thought back then—truly, deeply feared—we
Would destroy each other if you stayed?
You were nihilistically depressed, and I was

Really terrified one day I'd find you dead.
I couldn't think or sleep or read a line
Of Dryden for my course. The only answer
I could find was to get you somehow whole again.

It was my great gamble. As though we
Can survive roulette with life. You would
Go to San Francisco, there, supposedly
To think and grow, to come to know the sacred

Value of our love. I'd win you then.
You'd come back, beg forgiveness for
Your suicidal craziness, your fear and jealousy,
Quite capable of independence but

Choosing freely then to be with me. That was
My plan. So I forced you toward the plane,
Watched you board, heard the engines, first one
And then the other, roar, saw it taxi,

Speed along the runway, lift its nose,
Take flight, and in the vivid sky, stark as irony,
The wings leaned sharply to the south,
The craft veered slowly toward the west,

Grew smaller, vaguer, just a dot, and
Disappeared into a perfect, brilliant calm.

Jon Michael Miller

I watched the spot, a wilderness of blue,
As though my soul had gone along with you.

v

If I could have a single moment of my
Life to live again ... Certain acts
Create immutable identity, secure a fate,
Put to end a world. Unredeemable. What solace

Is there in forgiveness if the loss
Is permanent? A vanishing, sure as death,
A kind of homicide, born of vanity,
Illusion, and the pride of thinking

One deserves perfection. What if I had
Held you then and faced the turmoil? Hadn't you
Raced back to me, an act more real than words?
Would we be together even now? A compromise

For both of us, no doubt, but isn't that the deal
Real people make, accepting imperfection
As the fact of life? Why was I incapable of that?
A moment God, in His gracious trust, placed firmly in my

Hands to see it bungled, the hallowed gift
Betrayed? Yet time heaved on, my heart beat
Solidly, my breath in bursts of fog, the sky
A sea of azure emptiness, a void, a blinding calm.

vi

Five faded photos in an attic box, along
With two Point Reyes agates, without their luster
Ordinary sea stones now, but having
Symbolized in those amazing days the two of us.

One Ohio chestnut, innumerable exuberant refrigerator
Notes, that image of the swallow's dive, a burst
Of joy become a faded imprint of your lips upon a page, and
Finally in purple ink to mark a cherished line – my name.

I sat there on the narrow stairs with futile fragments
Of a past revived, unforgiving evidence
Of what I'd lost, and in my chest, the long familiar
Ache of irreversible mistake.

vii

To think of all these years gone by
And you as near my heart as breath itself.
You were to me no less than
Life defining. You never meant to be,

But here it is once more, a fact, ragged
As the sycamore I clambered up in springtime
As a boy. The rough, curled bark of
That old tree remains a kind of marker,

An emblem of what means most to me.
Like cold Ohio nights, strolling in the snow
With you, feeling of a single life,
An ageless fusion, a touch that joins all things.

Of spring and lying by the window, ivy
Tendrils creeping on the screen like veins,
Evening breezes washing over us like whisperings,
Benedictions for our soft embraces. Words,

I know, now as useless as the tears we shed.
Once we walked on Zuma Beach, waves
Like thunder, huge and crisp. How hard
I'd worked to free my heart from yours, and thought I had.

Those breakers weren't Columbus snow.
Nor was the Humboldt mist, the redwood
Grove where we lay rain drenched, shivering,
Wanderers and vagrants, lost to one another and the world.

Nor those mystic nights among the Alps,
A sea of clouds below, full moon glowing bright
Above majestic white capped peaks.
I listened to a joyous monk, my Master, a rose

Against his cheek, who taught of Krishna
And Arjuna. I was alone then, standing proudly in my
Hard-won strength, healed, I thought, and
Whole once more. Yet when I started sinking deep

Beneath the mantra's subtlest light,
Prana cool and thin as alpine air,

83

When all would widen out beyond the
Distant mountaintops, the moon and stars,

Afloat and full of bliss, I'd see ...
Your deep adoring eyes. And now,
The final moments coming near, I find myself
Afraid of death, remembering the circle of my life,

And ever,

At the center,

You.

~

Paige silently wept, leaning against André, who had placed his arm around her as if in an act of possession. No other response seemed forthcoming as Jocelyn lay the pages in her lap.

"Okay, let's get this over with," Erica said at last. "I'm upgrading Luke's poetic ability from a D minus to a C plus."

"I'd give him an A minus," André said, "at least."

Jocelyn handed a box of tissues across the coffee table. André took it, pulled one out and handed it to Paige, who was slowly recovering.

"Why the tears, Paige?" Jocelyn asked, not because she didn't sense the reason but because she wanted to provoke a response at this possible moment of truth.

But settled into André's embrace, Paige hid her face by dabbing at her cheeks.

"Probably don't need to ask," Erica said.

"He cherished her," André said reverently.

Erica smirked. "No shit, Dick Tracy."

"I'd like to hear Paige's response to this," Jocelyn softly insisted.

With his free hand, André reached and speared a chunk of honeydew with a toothpick. As he chewed, he nodded with confirmation of the fruit's deliciousness. Paige lay one tissue aside and pulled out several others. Finally, she faced her friends.

"It makes me sad, Jocelyn."

"Yes, we can all see that, but can you expand on that a little?"

"You don't have to play psychiatrist here, Joss," Erica said.

Jocelyn nodded. "Quite right, Erica. Sorry, a habit. Well, I for one cannot see this as other than a deeply sincere tribute to his love for you, Paige. André is quite correct – *cherished* is the perfect word."

"Yes, he loved me. I never doubted that."

"And it seems you loved him," Erica said. "At least for a time."

"Yes, I did. And not for a time. Always."

"What's the bit with the swallows?" André asked, withdrawing his arm from around Paige's shoulders. "I didn't get that."

"It's from a poem, dummy," Erica said. "Wallace Stevens."

"What was the line again?"

Jocelyn found the spot. "*Consummation of the swallow's wings.*"

"What's it mean?"

"Doesn't matter what it means," Erica said. "It's just pretty, that's all."

"Must mean something," André said. "What's it mean, Paige?"

Finished with the tissues, Paige said falteringly, "It's something we did. We had this little apartment we called the Hideout, and the property bordered a big, open field. And we'd go out there sometimes after dinner and throw a Frisbee around, and when the sun started going down, we'd lie on our backs in the grass and look up at the swallows." She smiled at the memory. "They were amazing, twirling around like they were consummating day with night. At least that's what I thought when I read 'Sunday Morning.' I remember lying there with Luke, watching them."

"They were probably catching mosquitoes," Erica said.

Paige smiled grimly. "Yes, probably. Or moths."

"Swallows are nasty birds," Erica added.

"Why do you say that?" André asked.

"Because my mom put out boxes on our backyard fence for bluebirds. The swallows used to chase them out, use the boxes for themselves. We didn't want the swallows, we wanted the bluebirds, then we eventually took the boxes down and..."

"All right," Jocelyn interrupted. "So do we all understand Luke's reference to swallows? Can we proceed?"

"Aye, aye, *Capitan* Consolo," Erica said.

"Oops," Jocelyn said, "there I went again, didn't I? Playing psychiatrist. Apologies. Are you okay, Paige?"

"Waiting for the gallows trapdoor to open."

"I think we all get the idea here," André said. "Luke loved Paige. I highly recommend the melon." He speared another chunk.

"It's all right, André," Paige said. "Ask what you want, Jocelyn."

"Well," Erica jumped in, "it's pretty damn clear Luke never got over his idea about a Grand Passion, as Joss refers to it. Never got over you, Paige."

"Yes, I always knew that, felt it."

"I'm curious about that roulette game he played with life," Jocelyn said. "Apparently he was aware he was taking a big chance sending you to me."

"So going out west, that was the gamble?" André asked. "You met that surfer boy, and game over? Goodbye, Luke."

"No. He put me on that plane New Year's Day. Then he drove out to see me over Easter break. He had a VW van with a mattress in back, and curtains, and we drove up to Yosemite and camped."

"Did he take you back to Ohio?"

"I was waiting for him to ask. But he didn't."

"Did you tell him about Jesse?" Jocelyn asked.

"No. I felt Luke was testing my strength, my stability, measuring my neediness. I didn't pass, not that he put it in so many words. Just that he needed more time, to focus on his courses."

"His second fatal play at the roulette table," André said.

"Isn't this when meditation got involved?" Jocelyn asked.

"Oh, yes. We started TM before I left Columbus, in November. I wanted to go to an introductory lecture; there were posters around campus. But we couldn't start that time because there was a two week restriction on pot use, so it wasn't until the second time they came to campus that we started. Luke poo-pooed the whole thing but decided to take the little course with me, and we stopped using pot, which we only did once in a while. We started meditating together. He saw I liked it, and thought it might bring us together again, out of my depression, but I was too far gone. We did it, but I'd just sink into the blues afterwards."

"So, what's this meditation stuff have to do with the price of beans?" Erica asked.

"Kind of everything," Paige said.

"Go on," Jocelyn said in her professional voice. "I don't remember meditation being very important when you came out to me."

"No, it wasn't. I just thought it was cool. I started smoking pot again with Jesse, and thought *everything* was cool – Maharishi, Gaskin, surfing, the city, the music, all your advice, Jocelyn – all one giant coolness, TM just one point of interest among many."

"But didn't you just say," asked Erica, "that meditation was everything?"

"Yes. I got this amazing letter from Luke. He'd had a mind blowing epiphany about Maharishi after he read his book, a translation of the *Bhagavad-Gita*. He became a convert and wrote that it was the way out of our troubles. When he came to visit that Easter he was devout, and when we were together that week, we didn't do dope, just meditated every morning and evening, and he showed me a yoga routine, very basic, that he'd learned in an advanced course he'd taken one weekend."

"So he converted you?" Erica asked.

"No. That's just it. I told him there were a lot of other paths to happiness, that TM was groovy and all, but not exclusive. There were other gurus and methods all leading to the same place. I'd become part of the counterculture, all embracing, I guess. It might have been one of the reasons he didn't want me to go back to Columbus, and one of the reasons I wasn't sure either, his being so absolute about TM."

"And Jesse was one of the cool things," André said.

"Yes. The whole scene at that time."

"The scene *was* fantastic," Jocelyn said in affirmation.

"Yes, Jocelyn, and you were pushing me right into the thick of it."

"I thought it was the cure, Paige, like being with sweet André had been for me."

"So," Erica said, "he went back to his new religion, and you went back to Jesse."

"Yes, him among others, I have to admit, as things progressed. I was never attached to Jesse. For one reason he wouldn't allow it. He was partaking of all the opportunities that magic place offered, and he encouraged me to do so also. I was hesitant but realized I wasn't in love with him, I was in love with the sex. Holy cow, that sounds crass. But I learned to separate sex and morality. It was just another bodily function, or need, or coolness, or whatever."

"Like a good honeydew," André said, stabbing the last in the bowl.

"Or a good Caribbean curry," Jocelyn added.

"Now you speak-a-my language," André said. "Caroline's lunch was really something."

"And gone the myth of the Grand Passion?" Jocelyn asked Paige.

"Yes, and my dependence on Luke. When he left me that Easter, I was okay. Changed, but okay. I had the whole wonderful world to fall into. He just told me, no matter what, keep on meditating. He figured with some growth in consciousness, I'd evolve out of my indiscriminate folly."

"Which, apparently, you did, right?" Erica asked. "You now live there in Iowa with a bunch of yogis, gave up meat, wear saris, twist yourself like a pretzel."

Paige smiled. "A lot more than that, Erica."

"Yeah, apparently flying around in the clouds."

"No, Erica. It's all about the development of consciousness, to see deeper, to act more effectively."

"And levitating? Give me a damn break."

Paige leaned forward. "Yes, I know that must sound weird, and it's where our movement veered away from the mainstream, took up a cultish look. But what so enthralled Luke back then and utterly eluded me is the idea of expanding one's consciousness. I just thought it was like for peace and love, but what Luke discovered in Maharishi's book was the possibility of developing one's mind, not just relaxation and getting rid of stress. And he thought if we both did that..."

"Get smarter, you mean?" André asked.

Paige smiled. How could she not at André? "I guess you could put it that way. And Luke envisioned it as a way for us to get back together. You see, he so identified with Arjuna in the *Gita*, a good man facing an insurmountable problem, that..."

"Meaning *you*," André said. "You were the insurmountable problem?"

Another smile. "Yes, me. It seems I've been his lifelong insurmountable problem. But please don't make me give you all an introductory lecture about my belief system. Just that Krishna appeared to poor, suffering Arjuna and gave him a method to expand his consciousness and thus allowing him to find the solution."

"By meditating?" Erica asked.

"Yes, by growing one's consciousness. But back then, Luke was eons ahead of me spiritually. Catching up just took me much longer than he ever imagined."

"From his poem," Erica said, " it certainly doesn't sound like Luke solved the problem, so it appears that Lord Krishna decided not to show up in his case."

"Please, Erica," Jocelyn said. "Let's not belittle each other's beliefs. Sooner or later we all enter the realm of faith. Even no faith is a kind of faith." She turned to Paige. "But I remember you suddenly taking off for Columbus not too long after Luke came out here. Packed most of your things, like you might stay with him, like you'd made your decision."

"That was because I saw the Ohio State protest riots on TV. Then Kent State where students actually got killed. The National Guard had closed the Ohio State campus too. I was scared for Luke and suddenly felt an overwhelming need to be with him again. I didn't call him or anything, just used my return ticket and went back."

"I need a bathroom break," Erica said.

"Yes, good idea," Jocelyn agreed.

~

"This story would make a good flick," André said, smiling at Paige as they walked upstairs together. "You okay, kiddo?"

"Just a little shell shocked is all. This is really reaching back into the depths. It's only for Jocelyn. She seems so persistent about it."

"She doesn't look well to me, Paige. What do you think?"

"Just a bit older, of course. It was a long trip out here for her."

"Yeah, maybe that's it. So we'll get you through this, your karmic debt, or whatever. Satisfy Joss's curiosity. *Luke's Revenge* we'll call the movie."

They stopped at her door.

"And," he added softly, moving closer, "I really enjoyed last night."

She pressed a finger to his lips. "Shh. Let's speak no more of that."

She slipped inside, and André wandered off to his own bedroom.

13

In her room Jocelyn's back was killing her so she popped a handful of Advil capsules and stretched out on her bed, the ceiling fan sending down waves of coolness. The discussion wasn't going well. The chronology of the events was not the point. The point was – the elephant having migrated from the gazebo to the chat alcove – what had happened between Paige and Luke, what had taken her from her Grand Passion to her so called *blues*. Jocelyn was sure she, herself, had not been responsible for Paige's eventual reemergence into life's *grooviness*. Yes, by shifting Paige's outlook, by endorsing her entering the counterculture, she'd led Paige to a solution but simply by diverting her from the real issue, not by resolving it, little more than Luke's technique of redirecting her attention. Paige's breakdown was a riddle that had annoyed Jocelyn from day one of Paige's appearance at San Francisco International. Paige had answered Jocelyn's probes by saying 'I don't know' so often that Jocelyn had simply given up and taken the last resort approach of calling Jesse.

Her own Grand Passion had ended clearly, no ambiguity whatever – Tony absconded with his family to Buffalo. End of story. But unlike Tony, Luke hadn't wanted it to end with Paige, and sending her to the West Coast was not intended to be a permanent breakup, but a reclamation. Yes, he'd lost the gamble, but that was due to something in Paige, something as yet undiscovered by Jocelyn. But was all this present recounting of events unearthing the hidden issue? It certainly didn't seem so. Paige admitted she knew that Luke loved her – *cherished*, the perfect word – had loved her always. Jocelyn had had every reason, however, to doubt Tony's undying love, but not so Luke's for Paige. His poem had proven that beyond all doubt.

Perhaps this group therapy would have to be changed to a private session with Paige.

Sometime later a knock on the door startled Jocelyn awake.

"We're waiting for you downstairs," Erica said. "Should we cancel the interrogation or are you coming?"

"Be right there. Sorry. Give me a minute."

"We're reconvening at the gazebo, Doctor Joss."

~

André and Erica were already soaking in the hot tub, the drone of cicadas in the background. The sound, the greenery, and the feel of the heavy August air pulled Jocelyn back to her childhood, the backyard of her parents' house on Mifflin Street, the play swing. In that innocent spirit, it hit her that maybe all this probing into another's psyche might not be ethically proper. It was for her *own* purposes, after all, not to cure Paige of anything. Paige had made her way in life. Maybe now was the time to back off, let it go as one of those enigmas all of us must accept as unsolved and unsolvable.

"Hey, Paige," André said when they resumed. "Do you remember those snapshots Luke talked about?"

Jocelyn felt pleased that André, not she, had asked the first question of this go round.

"Yes, André," Paige said. "I remember them all too well."

"Wouldn't happen to have the one at the beach handy, would you?"

"André," Jocelyn said as if to a naughty schoolboy.

André sat up straight. He wanted to protect Paige from what was coming. "Sorry, professor. How long does this have to go on, anyway? Couldn't we talk about a trip to the river tomorrow?"

"I have a request, Jocelyn," Paige said.

"All right."

"Well, I think I know where you're going with all this, yes, besides honoring Luke. I feel we're just dragging André and Erica along. maybe you and I should do this alone? You and I, privately?"

Jocelyn took a moment. "That might be a good idea. Turning to the two of them, "André, Erica, would you mind?"

"Now I'm curious," Erica said.

"Well, Erica," André intervened, "this isn't the *National Enquirer*. I get a sense that we're being excused to the billiard room. How's 'bout I beat the dickens out of you. Straight or eight, your choice, you're going down."

"Damn, if we must, André. Ha, look who's hustlin'."

"The loser buys a round of drinks at dinner."

"Thanks," Paige said. "I mean it, really, thank you, both."

The two outsiders, honoring what she was about to discuss with Jocelyn, left the gazebo for the rec room, drying themselves with bath towels on the way.

"I was thinking the same thing," Jocelyn said when they were alone. "This is between you and me. What is it you think I want to know?"

Alone with the elephant, they sat across from each other on the edge of the Jacuzzi, dangling their feet in the warm water. The shade protected them from the summer heat, birds singing, cicadas whining in unceasing unison.

"You want to know about my depression, back then with Luke."

"Yes, it's always been a great puzzle to me. I well understand clinical depression – it's part biochemical, can be treated, lithium, whatever – but it's not often cured by a mere change of scenery, as great as the city was."

"I don't think it was clinical depression."

"Paige, I have the feeling it was directly related to something particular between you and Luke. Call it chemistry. Something about that dynamic pulled you down. I understand the pressure you must have been under, abandoning your husband, leaving your way of life to be with Luke. Your words, 'bored with domesticity,' yet the fear of depending completely on him. That would explain a dark mood, but suicide? I don't see it. Was the threat of taking your life a way of somehow getting control of Luke?"

Paige gazed into the pool, into the froth as she spoke.

"Luke didn't need controlling, although he did come back from Lancaster after that first Easter apart feeling guilty about his attraction to Erica when he'd gone home. Erica was cool, cold to him, apparently; he might have slept with her again if she'd been interested. He broke down, said he'd understand if I left him. But where was I to go? And when I told him I loved him and held him like a mother would, he was so happy and relieved, said he'd love me forever. Said I'd saved him, that I was the one he'd been searching for all his life. All so ironic."

"Why do men think they have to confess their attraction to other women?" Jocelyn asked, observant of her old friend's body language. "Don't they know we never forgive them for that kind of crap?"

Paige's head was down, her mind lost in the foam.

"I really had no choice but to forgive him."

"What do you mean, no choice?"

"Because..." Paige covered her face with her hands.

"Because what?"

"Oh, my God! This is so difficult to say."

"Well, Paige, we've come a long way to get to this point. Don't worry, I'm not here to judge. Go ahead. Why was Luke's confession, as you say, ironic?"

Still hiding behind her hands, Paige said, "Because over that break, while we were apart, I slept with my husband."

Jocelyn stopped swishing her feet.

"Really."

"Yes," Paige slowly went on, letting her hands move to her knees and head still bowed, not able to look Jocelyn in the eye. "Luke had left me alone in that dingy little apartment, said he had to go home to visit his mother, who lived by herself. Actually, he'd invited me along, but I insisted I had to stay and study. The idea of meeting his family so soon made me uneasy. He tried to persuade me, but I just wasn't ready. I was miserable being there alone. I missed my little dog, and my house and garden. So I called Ted and asked if I could go over. We spent two days together mostly in bed, but he didn't ask me to go back to him. He'd found someone else."

"Did you want to go back to him permanently?"

"I was confused. I loved Luke, but I was in over my head. Luke was so in love with me, I felt like I was being buried under an avalanche."

"So when he made his confession about Erica, you didn't reciprocate with a confession of your own."

"I'd have lost everything. And it would have crushed Luke. By that time, he was all I had. And in a way it was my fault for not going with him. And he was really magnificent. And I really loved being with him. It was exactly as he wrote, except..."

"Except?"

Paige gave Jocelyn a look, her large, tearful eyes filled with grief.

"Except I wasn't loyal to him. Besides my husband, there were other episodes. There was a guy in the English Department, a real intense scholar type, Miles, and he slept with a lot of the women – highly in demand as straight men are in English departments. And he would give me these looks, all the time, these looks, in meetings, across classrooms, always looking at me. He was attractive and into..."

Again her gaze turned to the water.

"Into what, Paige?"

"Ropes, handcuffs, blindfolds. It was common knowledge about Miles. I was curious."

"I see."

"You know, Jocelyn, Luke was kind of considerate and, face it, conservative. Anything aggressive was just not him."

"In bed you mean."

"He never just took over and did what he wanted. I'd only had intercourse with my husband before Luke, and Luke had been with a lot of women, but in a way I was more experienced than he. I mean we did some kinky things – we went to a dirty Swedish movie once, very tame back then – and he took some Polaroids of me out in the woods, and once he asked me to undress for him while he watched outside through the window. He was vigorous and attentive to me, but..."

"Too considerate?"

"Yes, to really finish. I mean *really* finish the way Miles had, so, Jesus, even though Luke and I had great sex, he had limitations, out of respect for me, I guess. He never just let go and did his thing."

"And you couldn't tell him, let him know what you wanted?"

"I thought he'd think me too slutty. Yes, that's the word. *Slutty.* We were in a Grand Passion, and he wouldn't do anything he thought might degrade me."

"Like rough you up a little?"

"Well, yes. Let himself go." She looked up as if miffed. "You know what I'm talking about, don't you, Jocelyn? You used to tell me about sexual freedom and exploration. You and Brien."

"But you always seemed shocked, even though I assumed you did everything with Jesse, and the others."

"I did, but I hid it. Didn't want to admit it. Like I was in a closet, so to speak, like gays used to be. I was ... oh, God ... a sex addict. I admit it. A sex addict."

Not wanting to show her surprise, her shock, Jocelyn nodded reflectively. She thought Paige's secret might have been more along the lines of an abortion.

"And you were never loyal to Luke?" she asked as Paige twirled a strand of hair and stared down at her knees.

"I wanted to be what he thought I was. Didn't think he'd understand what I actually was, wouldn't accept it. But I was weak. In a way, sex with Luke, as good as it was, an act of love every time, left me wanting, left me hornier and hornier. I guess he was 'soft core' compared to 'hard core.'"

"And you wanted 'hard core'?"

"Yes, sometimes." She looked up at Jocelyn again, challenge in her eyes. "Didn't you?"

Slow to respond, Jocelyn said, "I did, Paige. Hard core can be good."

"Yes. The Stones instead of Rachmaninov."

"Absolutely. Both, depending, and everything in between."

They chuckled together, another barrier down.

"And then, as things progressed, the more I bugged him about his looking at other girls. Jesus, we weren't wearing bras back then. And I'd seen him scoping things out, hassled him endlessly about wanting to sleep with this one or that, plagued him with my jealousy."

"He *did* tell you he might have done it with Erica. So you had some reason."

"But deep down I knew he was all mine."

"Sure, Paige. We call it projection. Projecting your own impulses or unwanted traits onto others. This seems a classic case."

"It was horrible what I was doing. Making poor Luke think I was exclusively his and blaming him for what I, myself, was actually doing. I can't tell you how hideous it all was, and drew me downward, so that finally I really was suicidal. I fell into these bouts – we called them my traumas – when I wanted to end it all. It scared Luke out of his wits. And he'd ask me what was wrong, and – my God, Jocelyn – I'd tell him it was because he was cheating on me, sleeping with other women, and I know, and knew back then, it was all a demented lie."

She'd changed from melancholy reflection to letting off steam.

"Like you were driving him to break up with you?"

"He was right to force me to leave. One hundred percent. I would have killed myself. Did he ever tell you the time he tricked me about that?"

"About committing suicide?"

A monarch butterfly alighted near Paige's knee, apparently for a sip of water from a tiny puddle. It waved its wings mildly as it drank. She watched it, smiled. Observing it, she drifted back in time...

...flashback to November, 1969

95

Naked, Paige lay on her stomach in bed, her head buried in a pillow.

"What's wrong now?" Luke said, just out of the shower.

"Nothing."

"Don't say nothing. It's always something. What is it this time?"

"I know you want to go to bed with Rose Ann."

"Stop it. I'm sick of this."

"I just want to die."

He sat down beside her. "You keep saying this, weeks now. I'm beginning to believe you."

"I do." She sobbed. "I really do."

"God damn, how did it ever come to this? Don't you realize what we have – had, I mean? How could you let this happen?"

"I can't trust you. You're always looking at her, looking, looking."

"It's only you I care about, but you're driving me crazy."

"I just want to be dead."

She heard him sigh, felt his hands massaging her back.

"Okay, Paige. Why don't we do it together?"

She paused. "What?"

"Together. Now. Dead, you say? Let's do it."

"Really?"

"Yes. I'm nothing without you. And I can't bear seeing you like this. Let's do it."

His thumbs moved on her spine.

"But, how?"

"In the bathroom. The gas heater. We'll turn it on but not light it. Come on. Enough of this misery."

"Yes," she said. "Oh, yes."

She let him pull her up, lead her there. He spread his damp towel on the floor, closed the door, nudged her downward, stretched out beside her. She heard the hiss of the gas. Whiffed the fumes. He held her close, his body warm, a comfort. She closed her eyes. Yes, this was good. How she loved him! She inhaled as he held her to his strong, warm body. She felt dozy.

Then, a suddenly flurry as he pulled away. The hiss ended. He yanked open the door, gripped her under her arms, dragged her out and onto the bed. He flung the windows up, opened the door. Frigid winter air swept through, chilling her. She quaked from the cold, coughed. He threw a blanket over her, coughing too.

After a while, she realized where she was, what had just happened, opened her eyes. The threat over, the stench of gas gone, he was closing the windows. She lay quietly. He was at the stove, stirring pudding, she smelled the chocolate.

"That was close," he said, his naked back toward her as he stirred. He poured the pudding into cups. Came over to her, put a spoonful to her lips. She slurped it up, a heavenly taste, warm, smooth. After it was all gone, he lay down beside her, kissed her, touched her breasts, her nipples. She tingled all over. They made love.

"You are such a mystery," he said afterwards, holding her. "But I can't take this anymore. I wanted to see if you were really serious. And you are, would even take me along with you. I can't help you. I don't want to go there. I need to be by myself. And you must do what you must do. But know this. I love you, and I always will. But life or death? – that must be your decision, yours to do alone, dear Paige."

~

The butterfly had remained as if it were part of the conversation.

"You really would have done it, Paige?"

She looked up at Jocelyn. "Yes."

"And he got you into counseling."

"The university had a program. I talked to a man a few times, but never told him about my real addiction. I stopped seeing him because he was drawing me somewhere I didn't want to go, but might have."

"God, Paige, you mean into bed?"

"Onto his couch, at least. But even *I* knew how out of bounds that was."

The two women stared at each other across the hot tub. The butterfly lifted, flitted about in the gazebo and returned to the open air.

"Is that enough, Jocelyn? Do you understand now?"

"Just let me ask you this. Were there men in the city you didn't tell me about?"

"Yes, there were. I lived in secret, Jocelyn, even from you. Secrecy about this subject has been a life history with me, until this moment. I did just about everything a girl could do. There was a book shop on North Beach. They made films in the back, a hundred dollars. Jesse and I..."

Jocelyn interrupted. "I was curious, but don't need to know the details. You have every right to your private life. It's just even with all our mutual soul searching back then, I felt I really didn't know you."

"I didn't let you. But with all your sympathy and understanding, you helped me at least survive with myself."

"And has all the meditation, your community, helped you overcome your addiction?"

"Do addicts ever overcome their addictions, Jocelyn?"

"Few, but with effort some manage to control it, at least."

"Well, I'd like to tell you I have, but this is the time for truth, isn't it? So I can't say I have overcome it, entirely. Sometimes the urge is just overwhelming. I see a beautiful man and..."

More silence. More staring at frothy currents.

"And Luke never knew, never suspected, Paige?"

"I couldn't tell him. Just couldn't."

"So he thought you were psychotic. He must have been surprised at your seeming recovery from depression when you were in Frisco."

"Guess he thought being with you worked, and it had, but in reverse to what he'd hoped for. Ironically, the distraction actually became my reality. I simply had to learn to accept it. And in that playground and with your encouragement, it became easy to be what I was. What, I guess, I still am at my core."

"And Luke stumbled along through his whole life bewildered, wondering what had happened to his Grand Passion."

"Luke has been my greatest sin, Jocelyn. I don't know how I'm going to deal with that karma finally hitting me, which I guess, is this weekend."

"Paige, come on. You really buy this karma ideology?"

"Luke's letters and your having called this meeting, Jocelyn, are pretty strong evidence in my eyes. Plus, in the Vedas karma ranks as a natural law, right up there with gravity."

"Okay, it's a religious thing. Can't make any headway with that – not overcoming religion is a natural law in psychoanalysis."

Silent, staring downward, they stirred the water with their feet. Cinnamon, the calico cat with a little red collar, wandered in, its tail straight up. Closest to the entrance, Paige smiled, reached down and stroked it.

"But," Jocelyn eventually said, "somehow you ended up with Luke again, in Ohio, then back here in Lancaster."

"Yes, I laid even more misery on the poor guy. But need we go into it right now? I'm feeling exhausted. You, Jocelyn, are the only one I've ever told about this."

"I figured you went through a promiscuous stage in Frisco. Wouldn't have guessed about the films. But it never died down?"

"Not really." The cat rubbed its face against Paige's fingers. "But age has helped quiet things a bit. Along with the shear logistic difficulty of secret shenanigans. But it goes on, even at my age. The eyes see, the body responds. Someone new and strange and lovely, what might it be like...."

"Even in your Iowa ashram, Paige?"

"Yes, even there, sometimes. Not for a long while, for me. Meditation activates the senses, though. Makes you want to enjoy the pleasures of relative existence."

"I thought it was for the peace."

"During, yes. But afterwards, you're energized."

"And you're still beautiful. I'm sure that helps."

The cat moved on to Jocelyn, who stroked its back.

"Men still like me, at least," Paige said. "I'm glad to say. It's nice to be desired, chosen."

Jocelyn took a long breath as if an extensive trail had been blazed. "I've spent a lifetime wondering. Along with Luke. Thank you for revealing all this."

"Seems there's more to come with André's poem from Luke. But we won't go into what I've just confessed to you, will we, Jocelyn?"

"No, there's no need for that. But I would like to forge ahead. I'd like to understand André a little better."

"Good luck with that," Paige said. "I'm worn out. I'm going to my room and have a good cry."

"Me too. Not to cry, but my back hurts. Thank you, Paige, for confiding. Your secret is safe with me. I must say, I knew there was something, but I didn't expect ... hard core and porn flicks. You don't seem the type."

"We addicts are terrific actors. But Jocelyn...."

Their eyes met. "Yes, Paige?"

"There is one more thing you should know."

"Please."

The cat jumped up on one of the lounge chairs and peered upward at the wasp nest.

"It's something else I've never mentioned."

"That's fine. Go ahead."

"All right. About a year after my first marriage, I learned I probably wouldn't be able to have children. I had endometriosis. It's a condition that-"

"Yes, dear, I know what it is."

"Ted, my first, and I tried to get me pregnant, doctor's orders, but to no avail."

"It's not such a deep, dark issue, Paige."

"Just that Luke kept talking about having kids, a normal family. He was excited about the prospect, even talked about names. I felt he'd be so disappointed, so I didn't tell him."

"Did you think he'd reject you?"

"I don't know. I'd just found out, and felt humiliated, incomplete, damaged."

Jocelyn heaved a huge sigh. "Poor Paige. It might have been part of leading you to your addiction. Addiction often results from low self-esteem."

"I certainly didn't have to worry about birth control. Actually, I hoped I would get pregnant, didn't matter with whom. But I never did."

They sat silently, stirring the warm water with their feet. Cinnamon had curled up, eyes closed.

"It's so utterly ironic," Paige finally said.

"That word again? Why, Paige?"

"You see, Luke's core, to his very depth, was life affirming. He was so glad to be alive. Depression was his antithesis, and suicide unimaginable. When I was in that state, he had no idea what to do, kept going from empathy to pity to anger, to self-blame, to wit's end. 'How could you ever want to die?' he'd ask. 'Your not loving me any more hurts me, but not loving life? – Unacceptable.' Life denial was utterly repugnant to him, and at first I was almost his equal – in celebration of being alive, that is. Our Grand Passion, as you would have it. And when I turned downward, it was like the *ultimate* betrayal. He didn't want to go there, even though he loved me. 'I used to believe I'd do anything for you,' he told me, 'but you proved me wrong. I'll die defending you, but I won't go down with you for no reason.' And even when I went back to him from San Francisco, I knew he never forgave me. My cheating on him would have been difficult for him to overcome, but nothing to him, I realized, compared to my suicidal tendencies. He lost respect for me. Thought I was betraying something sacred."

Jocelyn was shaking her head. "You say 'utterly ironic' because he eventually succumbed to suicide himself."

"Yes. It kills me inside. And no family. I don't think I'll ever be really happy again."

"Well, he did save your life, didn't he? That trick with gas in the bathroom. Maybe you're not totally happy, but you're still alive, aren't you? And, after all, you did give him a precious gift, maybe the most precious."

"What gift is that, Jocelyn?"

"A lifelong love."

"Oh. Not realized, though."

"Maybe that's the only way it can exist – in one's imagination. But now that you've told me, everything fits into place. Thank you for this, Paige."

"I'm glad, Jocelyn. I can't tell you how much you helped me back then. I was very close to death, very close. And you're right, Luke saved my life, in a weird sort of way. First, that night in the bathroom, then by sending me to you."

"Close to death," Jocelyn said, "from the crushing weight of true love. But in spite of the weight, Luke helped you, too, don't you think?"

"He helped me so many times. When I got down, I thought of him. When I got desperate, I ran to him. I just couldn't bear to see his hurt. I just couldn't. I rather he'd simply thought of me as a frivolous, crazy bitch from the very beginning, just a horny house-wife for a meaningless tryst. He wasn't like the four of us. Things didn't roll off him."

14

In her room Jocelyn paced, stared out the window at the trees, sat on the edge of her bed and wept. She wept for Luke, for Paige, for Tony, for herself, for all humanity. She wasn't used to tears, her own at least, but here they were. Her life path had been a march of toughening up to life's verisimilitudes. It seemed all desperately sad. After Tony, she'd rolled her energy into a hunk of gristle and held on, determined to understand. After all the hard work and resolve, she had finally come up empty, sitting here feeling nothing but un-determined grief. She'd shoved her sadness back until this moment. Paige had diverted her own attention from it, and Erica and André didn't feel it at all. Oh, to be like them!

Then there had been Luke, who felt it, who hadn't let it go, who saw it for what it was and bore the cross honestly. He died a believer in a perfect love, a sufferer of that belief but never its be-trayer. Luke – steady, enduring, sensible, decent, bearing a wound he'd neither comprehended nor ignored. His true love had cheated on him, and worse, had more than flirted with the idea of suicide –

a dreadful but simple truth he'd had to bear for a lifetime. And not knowing the real truth, he could only see it as his own inadequacy, for when Paige had been parted from him, she regained her zest for life. He could only have thought that for some reason, despite his total love for her, he wasn't what she wanted, hadn't been good enough, so distasteful to her that she wanted to die to escape from him.

Paige hadn't been worthy of him from the very start. He'd been a plaything for her, an object of her addiction whom he'd mistaken for the love of his life. Yes, when this playgirl ran into him, she was certainly in over her head. Luke in *under* his.

Then, Jocelyn's final embarrassment – of Erica's *instinctive* understanding of Paige's nature from the very start, an understanding that, with all Jocelyn's empathy, life experience, and training in psychology, had eluded her for decades, until this very afternoon. Yes, humiliating.

André and his ilk would have been far better toys for Paige than Luke, who, like Jocelyn herself, had simply never seen her for what she really was. But then, as she'd just confessed almost boastfully, she was adept at camouflage. And all that love Luke poured over her had trickled down the drain of her narcissistic need.

His writings showed that he'd sensed it, finally. But surely for the wrong reason. The pain, however, must have gone just as deep. So he'd written his parting thoughts and died alone on a deserted beach, no family to mourn his passing.

After more weeping, Jocelyn dried her eyes, took two pain pills, lay down and went to sleep.

~

Down the hall in her small guest apartment, Paige also wept. For her, the tears flowed from self-contempt. Luke had been the only man she'd ever truly loved. How she wished she could have been worthy of him! But no matter the ideas of sexual freedom that the era had been swimming in, she had exercised her uncontrollable needs but never felt free. She understood Luke's moral fiber, knew that every time she cheated, every time she returned a seductive smile to another man, or issued one, guilt came attached like the remora fish that follow sharks around. She succumbed to her urges simply because she couldn't resist. Facing her object of desire, she became a kind of zombie, unattached from her moral sense, driven to the pleasure she received, leaving it behind for bits of time after the hours or the weeks of wallowing in it, only eventually to return to the realization that she was a pariah. Utterly alone. True love didn't work. Celibacy didn't work. Self-control didn't work. The only mental construct that gave her any consolation whatever was the one that told her, "You are what God made you. You are what you are. Just try not to hurt anyone again." But it was false consolation. She had, indeed, hurt Luke, mortally, it seemed.

She recalled the care with which he'd first got into it with her, him looking right at her and saying, "This isn't simple. Others are involved. We must make a committed decision." And she agreeing. It should have ended there, having never begun. She'd been married, no serious intentions about giving Ted up. But that kiss in the doorway, the beauty of Luke's gaze, of his desire for her, of a kind of love she'd never received before. Desire for her, certainly, but that adoration, the sense of danger, the shear seriousness in his eyes – never. She believed it until he'd left her alone that Easter break. And after her weekend back in her house with Ted, she realized what she'd fallen into with Luke. Ted was light, like the others, but Luke was a mountain. And with his confession and appeal for forgiveness, her guilt had been too much to bear. And the months of blissful denial had led down a path to the deepest darkness she'd ever known. She'd wanted to die from its burden, and nearly had.

And – oh, God – by giving her up, by sending her away, he'd saved her.

Luke had tried everything to recover her. She'd felt worse for his efforts, strived to be what he wanted, but by the time of the darkest hour, she was irretrievable to him. He was entirely correct to have sent her off. And the odds of winning his gamble, which he couldn't have known? – Absolute zero. He couldn't have been more mistaken than by thinking she could give him the pure love he sought and had thought he found.

Paige wept for her lifelong failure, and if she had wanted to spare herself the pain on Luke's face at her telling him the truth, she felt that sting at this moment with an almost unbearable anguish. Through the blur of her tears, she gazed at the picture of Guru Dev.

"Forgive me in your divine mercy," she muttered as her tears flowed. "Forgive me, dear Lord."

15

After their fifth game of eight ball, backed by the Eagles' Greatest Hits, Erica and André placed their cues in the rack and settled on the leather sofa to finish their beers, "Desperado" playing at the moment. They sank into the couch's deep suppleness.

"Where'd you get so good at pool?" André asked.

"My brother taught me. It sure helped me score in gay bars."

"Don't picture you needing much help there. Where is your brother these days?"

"Died. Ancient history. Car accident, drunk. The Manheim Pike, that sharp curve just past the Petersburg Quarry. He was thirty-seven."

"Randy, too, your photographer. Had his own plane, you know, a little Piper Cub, crashed on the Ephrata Mountain, fifteen years now. Left me all his prints and negs, quite a collection. Before I looked through it, I didn't know the two of you did even more stuff after I left your photo session that day."

"So what? He kept all that junk, huh?"

"Made a photogenic couple, you two, with that remote control."

"All right, André. Your point being?"

André smiled mysteriously, went to the video consul and opened a drawer. He returned with a small oriental box, opened the lid and showed the contents to his guest. She took in the sight, looked at him and smiled.

"They're so perfectly rolled, like cigarettes."

"My daughter provides them for me. Care to partake?"

"Hmm, what about the others? Won't they be jealous?"

"They're well engaged in much deeper matters. Anyway, I'm sure Paige is high on yogi-ism, and as for Joss? No, I think this is a realm reserved exclusively for you and me."

"You're a real devil, aren't you, André." She lifted a joint from the box, inspected it, gave it a whiff. "Sure smells good."

He flicked on a lighter, held the flame toward her. She shook her head in happy resignation and inhaled deeply. When she handed it to him, he did the same.

"You do this very much?" she asked, propping her feet on the coffee table.

"Not very much. But I count it among life's great enjoyments. You? Out there where it's legal?"

"I do. Most days after work. I'm never bored when I'm high."

For a few minutes they passed the joint back and forth and listened to the music.

"Put on the Hotel California album," she said.

"*Oui, Madame.* You're every wish is my command."

When he returned, he took her in as she almost reclined, her long legs stretched out.

She glanced up at him. Their gazes held.

"What are you looking at?" she asked. "Are you checking me out?"

"Just been wondering if you're exclusively...?"

"What are you getting at, André? Did you take some Viagra today?"

He smiled. "Great memories die hard, is all."

"Jesus, how old are you?"

"A dynamic eighty-one."

"And coming on to a sixty-three-year-old lesbian. Some things never change, do they?"

"Hey, what makes you think...?"

Erica gave him a look.

"So do you still hit the gay bars, or are you out of the game at sixty-three."

"Occasionally I venture out, but I have to pay for what I really like."

"Young ones, eh? I'd think you're still sharp enough looking to..."

"And you and Muriel? Does she put up with...?"

The sounds changed to the lead song of the Eagles' album.

"Muriel and I understand each other."

She smiled. "Come here you gorgeous old man." She patted the seat beside her. He complied. They passed the doobie back and forth. "What do you think happens in this song, André?"

"What do you mean?"

"There in that gathering with the *steely knives?*"

"Needles. Drugs."

"Not an orgy?"

"That too, maybe," he said.

"Just always wondered about this song. Seems ambiguous. Who are the guys she *calls friends?*"

"She's a hooker. They're her johns."

"Yes, she tastes their *sweet summer sweat.* Why do they need *alibies?*"

"Her *friends* need to lie to their wives."

"Man," she said, "this weed is splendid. Where's your daughter get it?"

"I don't ask. Uh, here's a question for you, Erica? When's the first lesbian experience you ever had?"

"Now why would you want to know something like that, you pervert?"

"If I'm a pervert, why wouldn't I? So tell me."

She scoffed. "When Luke was living at my place, I joined a softball team, girls. There was one there named Nell, shortstop, came on to me, very cute, tough as nails. I'd been watching her, having fantasies. After practice one night, the others gone, we did it in the dugout. A lot of those girls were gay. Luke never had a clue about Nell and me."

"And was Nell on her knees, *abjectly?* Like in Luke's poem to you?"

Erica stared at him askance. "Dammit, André."

He stared back. "Well?"

"What are you up to, you old creepola? You think by talking dirty to a girl, she'll...?"

"Just a thought. I was watching you lean over the pool table in that swimsuit. Damn, you look good enough to eat!"

Erica huffed, glanced toward the stairs. "What if they come?"

"They're done for the day. Whatever they discussed, it wore them out."

She smiled, scoffed again. "Only you, André, with all our history, could.... Can you at least go up and lock the door?"

16

For dinner, Jocelyn drove the group to the Horse Inn, one of their old haunts on East Fulton Street. In those days the entrance to the converted stable and speakeasy had been down a narrow alley and up some rickety stairs, but the place had been renovated so they could now enter from the street. It was crowded and noisy as it had always been, this evening with a Dixieland quartet. In her green and blue sari, slim, shapely Paige drew glances as the hostess in flapper attire led the foursome to their reserved booth. Sleeves rolled, the bartenders wore striped vests, bowties and straw hats. To begin, Paige ordered the Burrata, Jocelyn the Farmer's Salad, Erica the Middleneck Clams, and André the Pork Lettuce Wraps. For their entrees, Paige the veggie plate, Jocelyn, not hungry, passed, Erica the Buttermilk Poached Chicken Breast, and André the Cornmeal Crusted Halibut along with Horse Inn's famous tenderloin tips on toast.

"Starved," he said, smiling, his excuse to the others, who were staring at him. The small carpenter's screw in his right earlobe glinted in the light.

He also ordered a bottle of the Jean-Luc Columbo Cape Bleue Rose. Paige and Jocelyn were happy with Earl Grey tea. The pre-season NFL game between the Redskins and the Giants playing silently on the large, flat screen TVs was interrupted by a news brief highlighting the Michael Brown killing in Ferguson, Missouri. Now, three weeks later the protests and burnings were still going on.

"I remember the Watts riots," André said. "Nineteen sixty-five."

"Yeah," Erica added, "not much has changed."

"What do we expect our cops to do," asked André rhetorically, "just let thugs take over the neighborhoods?"

The place was not quiet, making conversation difficult, no one willing to engage in an ongoing topic.

"You're on the chopping block tonight, André," Erica said as if to change the subject, "so you'd better have plenty of wine. It'll be a roast. We're going to skewer you."

"More wine at home," he answered. "Have a small cellar. We can all get hammered in honor of Luke's last poem."

"This isn't about anyone being skewered," Jocelyn said.

"Did you and Paige settle anything this afternoon?" Erica asked.

"Just talked a bit," Jocelyn said. "Nothing earthshattering."

"That's nice. And how about river rafting tomorrow?"

"The tubing place closed down years ago," André said, "but we can drive down to Otter Creek, douse ourselves at the falls. We can spy on the younger generation, all those gleaming young bods."

"Just make us sick with envy," Jocelyn said.

"I changed my flight," Paige announced. "Leaving tomorrow, noon."

The conversation stopped, all eyes on her.

"I think I've settled everything here."

"Why don't you and Erica go to the river, André?" Jocelyn said. "I'll see Paige off."

"Without you?" André answered. "No way. We'll all see Paige off."

"Any reason for the change?" Jocelyn asked.

"Reason? Uh, my husband called. But, André, I'd like to see some of your art before I go. What you've been working on, besides the amazing pieces you have on display."

"Yeah," Erica said with a leer, "your secret files."

"Nothing that can't be presented in a living room or a bank lobby. Secret files were Randy's trip. None of *my* shows has ever been closed down."

"I'm out of the loop on that reference," Paige said.

André explained how Randy's nude shots of Jocelyn had been expelled from the college's art gallery, causing a furious censorship debate in the local media.

The waiter arrived with the wine, which André sniffed and tasted like a connoisseur. He nodded his approval. Paige and Jocelyn held their hands over their wine glasses, so the waiter bypassed them. A weighty Peggy Lee lookalike came on stage, shifting the group's attention to her rendition of "Fever," which seemed strange with a Dixieland backup.

~

Later, after having changed into more casual clothing, the group gathered in the living room nook, André wearing a black Asian pajama outfit with Chinese lettering.

"You look like Hugh Hefner," Erica said.

"In the Hollywood Mansion with my harem," he added, eyes twinkling.

"You wish," Jocelyn countered.

He sat with Erica on one sofa, Jocelyn and Paige facing them on the other across the roughhewn coffee table on which sat a bottle of New Zealand rose from his collection along with tea mugs, accoutrements, a bowl of caramel chocolates, another of pretzel nuggets, and bottles of chilled Lititz Springs water.

"Hey," Erica said. "Before we get to Luke's thing to André, I'd like to catch up on Paige's odyssey, since she's leaving us. Don't need confessions, but last we talked, Paige, you went from Frisco to Columbus because of the protest riots. I know you later came here to Lancaster but there's a gap. What happened in between? Was your arrival in Ohio one of those running-through-the-airport-into-each-others-arms reunions?"

"Yeah," André added, seeing an opportunity to put off his own exposure, "you said Luke didn't know you were coming. Must'a surprised the hell out of him."

Paige recalled that moment...

...flashback May, 1970

After taking a cab from the airport, Paige was shocked to see the campus under lockdown with National Guard troops manning checkpoints, soldiers in military trucks, helicopters overhead. At Luke's shabby rooming house, tired from the travel time, a long stopover in Chicago, she lugged her backpack up the stairs to room number three. Suddenly she had second thoughts about having come. She waited. Four in the afternoon, a Donavan tune playing in the next room, she gathered her courage and knocked. And there he was, at first sleepy-eyed, then his eyes widening in shock.

"Paige!"

He stared.

"Hi, Luke."

"My God! You're back."

"Yes. Don't I get a hug?"

He grabbed her to him, gripped her, the faint scent of sandalwood in his ragged hair.

"Oh, Paige."

A young bearded man started pulling a bicycle up the stairs.

"Come in, Paige," Luke said, relenting from his embrace.

The efficiency, a mini kitchen at one end, was a mess, papers and texts on the unmade bed. The door closed, he looked at her, his delighted expression changing gradually to puzzlement.

"Who's Swanson?" he asked looking at the army jacket she was wearing, the letters stenciled on.

"Oh, just a friend. I saw the campus on TV. Had to come."

"Well, take that thing off, relax. You look exhausted, but the most beautiful sight I've ever seen."

She knew what he was thinking – that she'd finally realized the error of her ways and had come back to reclaim their past. But he was right about one thing – she was exhausted.

"I'll make you some tea."

He cleared some clothes and books from a frayed easy chair. Coat off, she sank into it. As he bustled about in sweats and tee shirt, they went over the details of Jocelyn's wellbeing, of Paige's trip, of her hippie existence. He hovered over her as if absorbing her presence. Seated on a kitchen chair, he filled her in on the campus happenings, the school closed, students gone home early from the term with passing grades, his disappointment with how the administration and faculty had handled the protests, and his ongoing interest in Eastern philosophy.

"Still meditating?" he asked.

"On and off."

He grimaced, then nodded.

"Anyway, you're here."

"Yes. I'm here, and I want you to hold me."

Later, naked, in tangled sheets, they lay together.

"So, who's this Swanson from the U.S. Army?"

"Oh, a friend. Nothing to worry about."

"Now I'm worried."

"Jesse's only recreational. Nothing like us."

"Jesse? So you...?"

She couldn't look at him, stared at the ceiling.

"Yes, but...."

Silence. He moved away from her a little. A fly buzzed around the light fixture.

He rose, went into the bathroom, closed the door. Though she'd had plenty of time to have planned for this moment, she'd subconsciously, perhaps, avoided it. Now, no plans, just the truth.

Back in a bathrobe, he sat on the easy chair.

"Should'a figured. Somehow I thought ... wishful thinking, I guess."

"It's nothing serious, Luke. Haven't you been into anything? All those women in the Department?"

"No. Only waiting. For that moment we just had at my door. But...."

Aware of what he was feeling, she pulled a sheet up over her, gritted her teeth.

"I was lonely," she said. "And you sent me away like you were finished with me."

"Sure, Paige. Totally understandable. So...."

In his silence, she waited, knowing the truth would pierce his awareness like a knife.

"So, why are you here? Why did you come back?"

"Impulse. I saw the riots on TV. I was worried about you."

It was a conversation with large gaps as if wheels were turning in Luke's mind.

"I see," he finally said. "Uh, so where do we go from here? What does this mean?"

110

"It means I had to see you. And here I am. Aren't you glad?"

"Yeah, sure. It's just that...."

"Jesse is not serious, Luke. Didn't you get involved with anyone?"

He scoffed. "No, I told you. Just memories of you, some crazy hopes."

"You can tell me. I'll understand."

"There's nothing to understand." He was clearly flustered at her implication. "Sorry. No, no one. I was waiting."

"Jocelyn said you must have known. That you wanted me to move on."

"Joss said that? That I wanted you to sleep with someone named Jesse Swanson from the U.S. Army?"

"That you wanted me independent. You knew I'm not a nun. Jocelyn pushed me into life again. And now I feel strong. And I don't think I would feel this way without...."

She really couldn't say anything more. But she knew her reappearance wasn't exactly that precious moment he'd been waiting for.

He sighed, deeply, tragically. "This isn't what I hoped for, dreamed of, but it's a helluva lot better than your being dead. You had me really scared of that."

~

"I assured Luke it was just physical with Jessie," Paige said, hanging her head as if shaken by the memory. "Physical, nothing more."

"That must have eased his mind," Erica said.

"No." She felt her neck warming. "So we started catching up. I could tell he was hurt, but he tried to absorb my new attitude. He asked me a lot of questions about Jesse, and I kept assuring him that he was irrelevant, and...."

"Irrelevant?" Erica interrupted, oddly pursuing information given her earlier disinterest. "To Luke? He must have hoped his true love had returned to him, finally rehabilitated."

"Yes, Erica," Paige said, glancing at Jocelyn. "I guess he did feel that at first. That's exactly what he'd wanted to happen – me to return, whole, to pick up when things had been working for us, to realize how wrong I'd been to reject what we'd had, the beauty of it, to reject, well, life itself."

"Like you owed him an apology?" Erica asked.

"No, not that. He'd wanted me to understand, to comprehend the preciousness of what we'd found with each other, an affirmation of the unbounded beauty of being alive, and of true lovers being the personification of that. I think he might have forgiven my straying from him if I'd come back having realized my mistake, maybe begged him for forgiveness, ready to start over as we first were."

"Thus, the jackpot for his big gamble?" André asked.

"I guess so, but when he realized that wasn't exactly the situation – that I hadn't come to him realizing the egregiousness of my error – he wanted to understand my new viewpoint toward life. I explained that you, Jocelyn, had introduced Jesse to me, and that it was the City, the times, relaxing our attitudes toward relationships, and that I'd been alone, and he hadn't invited me back. 'I thought you had let me go,' I told him."

"So did he *absorb* the supposedly new you?" Erica asked.

Noting the sarcasm in Erica's masked accusation, Paige said, "I don't think he could have, but he tried to." She was determined to see this all through to the end although she'd thought it had ended with her afternoon privacy with Jocelyn.

"Highly doubt you'd be celibate out there," André noted.

"What happened, simply happened. We were all doing it, part of the milieu. Free love, you know."

"Absolutely," Jocelyn backed her up. "Luke should have realized that."

"Thus ended the Grand Passion," André said. He drained his glass and refilled it.

"And how did that go?" Erica asked.

"Well, Erica, we hung out together. The campus was closed, trucks of soldiers, helicopters, the odor of tear gas in the air. Luke was disoriented by that and by me, and I saw him confused, weakened, and I suggested he drop out of grad school, come back to the West Coast with me, enjoy the vibes."

"The idea being you'd be there as a couple?"

"Yes, I suppose he thought so. I did too. He said he was fed up with how the university administration handled the protests, how none of these renowned scholars knew what they were doing, and I told him how fantastic California was, and after a lot of discussion he accepted my plan. I thought I could drag him in to a different awareness, like Jocelyn had done for me. I wanted to liberate him, I guess. So he gave all his students A's, submitted his resignation, and we drove out west in his camper."

"Lovers," André said.

"Very much so. I loved Luke. But things had changed. He didn't like that I'd been with someone else. He was jealous, his confidence broken. We weren't as close as we'd been. We stayed with Jocelyn, and Luke started looking for work, and – I find this hard to explain – but I started missing Jesse, and when Jesse called me at Jocelyn's and said he needed to see me, gosh, I had Luke drive me over to his place near the beach, had Luke wait for me outside thinking I intended to break it off with Jesse, but...."

"Don't tell me," Erica broke in while chewing a chocolate.

"It was so intense seeing Jesse again. He was all broken up and I felt sorry and needed more than the ten minutes I'd promised Luke. So I went out and told Luke to go back to Jocelyn's and I'd call him."

"How long?" André said. "An hour?"

"Two weeks."

"Damn!" Erica said.

"It happened a couple of times," Jocelyn broke in. "She'd call my place for Luke to go pick her up. They stayed with me for a week or two, then she'd go off to Jesse again."

Erica nodded wisely. "Luke must have been a barrel of laughs to have around, right, Joss?"

"That was when you visited, Erica, remember?"

"When you watched the *brutal* sunset with him?" André asked.

"Yeah, I knew he was hurting. And I thought, 'yes, love hurts, doesn't it?'"

"Luke hung around, pining," Jocelyn said, "looking for a job, found one as a waiter at a retirement hotel, which he soon quit. He was messed up. But he kept true to his meditation thing, tried to get me to start."

"Mustn't have been a very effective salesman," André said. "Start TM and you'll be as happy as me."

Erica snickered, took a sip of wine.

"He came up with one last plan," Jocelyn said. "He told me about it. Maharishi was holding a course up north in Arcata – Humboldt, the college there. Luke believed if he got Paige into meditation full scale, it could reunite them in the way he wanted, like it had been at first."

"Wait," Erica said. "Weren't you meditating with him when you were together, Paige?"

"Yes, but Jesse and his friends were into pot and acid."

"So you were a spiritual seeker with Luke and a pothead with Jesse?" André asked.

"Pretty much."

"So I gave Luke Jesse's number," Jocelyn picked up the story, "and he called and persuaded Paige to join him on a trip up to Humboldt."

"Thus," André said, "the reference to being lost in the redwood mist, in his poem to you, Paige?"

Paige grabbed a pillow and hugged it to her chest. "Yes. His van broke down, and we left it at a garage and hitched. It's a long drive. We were in the back of a pickup most of the way, freezing. And when we finally got there we couldn't get in. No tickets. Luke didn't know we needed tickets. We saw Maharishi, though, when he came out of the auditorium and got into a limo. The people formed an aisle and handed him flowers. Luke was enthralled. I was annoyed that they charged admission. And I was wiped out from the trip. We had some blankets rolled up from the van, and found a place to sleep on a lawn, then in the middle of the night the sprinklers came on and we got soaked."

"This is goddam pathetic," Erica groaned.

André laughed. "Couldn't have got much worse, could it, Paige?"

Paige looked at Jocelyn as if waiting to be saved, but Jocelyn held back.

"Let's just say I wasn't very impressed with the TM movement," Paige said, irritation rising. "I was fed up with Luke's devotion to meditation. Wanted to get back to the free life with Jesse. I think Luke knew then it wasn't going to work for him – me, the California lifestyle. I realized it anyway. We hitched back, picked up the van and I asked him to drop me off at Jesse's, said I'd see him whenever."

"I remember the night he came back to my place," Jocelyn said. "He looked like the walking dead. 'It's over,' he said, stuffed his backpack, and left for home."

A silence ensued. André grabbed a chocolate.

"Bathroom break," Erica said, leaping to her feet.

17

When they reassembled, the tea refreshed, the wine half gone, Erica noted the obvious truth that somehow after Luke's tragic retreat from the West Coast and Paige on her way to her life as a flowerchild, somehow she'd ended up later in Lancaster with Luke again.

"How'd that come about?" she asked as if relishing Paige's obvious discomfort.

Paige took a deep, flustered breath. "After the summer went by, and I'd been hanging out in California, it seemed as if I was wasting my life. I stopped the drugs and decided to get my teaching assistantship back at Ohio State but they'd filled all their spots, so I went to the TM Center on Fremont Street and had my meditation checked. Then I flew back to Columbus. Home in Dayton with my parents I hung around with the meditators at the center there. From you, Jocelyn, I knew Luke had taken a high school teaching job at one of the schools around here in Lancaster County – Warwick, in Lititz – and he'd rented a cabin near a lake and was living alone, and I phoned him one night and asked him if I could come and visit. He said yes – I figured he would agree unless he'd found someone else, which he hadn't. I think he was still waiting for my transformation."

"Back to the Grand Passion, you mean?" André asked.

"The only thing that would have satisfied him was my realization of how wrong I'd been. He said he was saving his money for a TM teacher training course in Majorca, Spain, the next summer, which would have been '71. He'd been to several weekend courses and was really into it."

"Didn't I hear you say," Jocelyn asked, "that it was you who'd wanted to learn TM, that he just went along to be with you?"

"That's right, the first time. Why?"

"Kind of ironic that he was the one who really got into it and then seemed to be pulling you along. His immersion in it was influencing you, by example, correct?"

"Yes, I can't deny it." She restlessly backed into her corner of the sofa, tucked her stockinged feet under her, her face flaccid. She spoke as if reciting, staring at her palms turned upward in her lap. "His certainty that it was the way to go impressed me. Anyway, I called him from Dayton, and he picked me up at the bus station in Harrisburg, and we spent time together in his lonely little cabin with his dog Emily, and in the course of things I met his TM friends, and André, of course, who had become a legend with all the stories I'd heard. I was beginning to respect Luke in a way I hadn't before — his dedication and devotion and his intellect. He was on a single track to become a TM initiator, as TM teachers are called. Very serious, and I was going nowhere and realized he wasn't in love with me the way he'd been before...."

"Grand Passion mode," Jocelyn said.

"Yes, I guess. So much water under the bridge. It was different, and I wasn't as committed to TM as he was, hadn't recognized my *fatal error*, still pretty much on the lighter side of things, and I guess I was a little flirty with his friends."

"Right-o!" André said. "Quite enjoyed that flirtiness."

"And it pissed Luke off," Erica noted in unmasked satisfaction.

Paige's peaceful hands were now wringing. In a hurry to get all this finished, she went on.

"And I don't blame him for not liking it, and in the course of things he got really annoyed with me one night because I'd been very flirty with one of his TM friends. I pretended I didn't know what Luke was talking about. So he just up and left me, moved to his mother's place — a really lovely person, I might add — and I ended up brutally alone in that lonely cabin, and after I was sure he wasn't coming back, I took a cab into town to André's Candy Factory and knocked on the door. I remember it was raining really hard."

"And he *reluctantly* took you in," Erica said, smiling.

"Let's just say he took pity on me. I was soaked to the skin."

After a moment of fidgety, relieved silence, Jocelyn said, "That about brings us to Luke's poem to André. Your turn to read Paige."

"I've been doing a lot of talking," Paige said. "How 'bout you, Jocelyn? You read so well."

"Yes, you've been on the dentist's chair." Jocelyn put on her reading glasses, and after some rustling of papers, she read.

TULIPS TURNING
From Luke Shields to André Roulier
Upon my parting.

Today on an obligatory visit home, I looked
Your name up in the phone book. Didn't call,
I'm not sure why. You'd be glad to hear my

Voice. We would meet for lunch in some downtown
Quaint café and reminisce. Maybe I'm afraid

Of what you'll say, or lack the nerve to broach
The topic on my mind some forty years. Even
Then you would evade, sliding as you always did
Around unpleasantness. You wrote a chapter of
My life, you know? An episode that troubles yet.

I would ask, had I the fortitude, how well you really
Knew her. If you noticed that neither of her little toes
Ever touched the ground, mere dainty stubs
Resting on their neighbors. Or if she ever read
A poem to you. Or laughed, as raucous as a crow.

Or looked up at you in wonder like a child. Or
Gorged fresh chocolate pudding, not quite cool.
I would like to know if my love changed everything
For her, or if she went on just the same, as I could
Never learn to do, if the miraculous for me had been

Simply commonplace for her. I have no right to know,
Of course. But there's still a yearning need. I had
Left her, after all, finality, a crushing blow delivered
To myself, left her in my country cabin, packed
My battered suitcase, took my dog and fled. Hurt

And anger didn't mitigate my choice. I could have
Stayed, continued to endure. But what we'd had was
Gone, lost in a tangle of unacceptable experience.
She'd not come back to me to find what we had lost,
To renew a precious past, which had been my only goal.

The loss of miracle was permanent, though I held on.
She was with me now as fugitive, bonded only by
The habit of old days, quite ignorant of essence, but in
Desperate need of something solid, her loss about what
Path to take, oblivious to my groping to reclaim

Past unity. The seals were broken, betrayals much too
Deep to heal, she must have sensed, apologies absurd,
Appeals transparent tactics. And, horribly, I was soon
To see, she had become what I did not – could not – want.
So where for her to turn? Where but to my friend, part

Of our deep history, Jocelyn's past paramour, raved about
By all, especially me? And why should you refuse to take
Her in, she become a sensualist like you? And lovely as
A mountain laurel. And utterly abandoned. Could I have
Really thought you'd say, "I'm sorry, dear, but I'm his

Friend, in tune with what he feels for you, aware of all
His pain"? No, I never thought you'd give her up for
Something that abstract. And had our situations been
Reversed, I may have acted just as you, no power to
Resist delectability for a concept vague as friendship.

Wasn't that our natural, silent understanding, man to
Man, that no such code of honor would deter a spot
Of carnal pleasure? And if a morsel alienated us, well
Then, the tidbit paid us fully in delight, the cost incurred—
Our having avoided one another since that night.

My choice as well as yours. I couldn't face you in my
Shame, could not visualize your intimacy with her,
Your mutual skill at casual sex, her dire relief at finding
Someone so less serious than I, a burden lifted from
Her meager frame, a playful force who could rejoice

In what she had become. Your terms so easy, all
The pressure gone. Pleasure as a means to pass the time,
Love for one another not a bother, hedonism just
The cure. My question still remains, however. What
Might we discuss across a shaded lunchtime BLT?

Was it what she'd always done? Was our Grand
Passion really nothing more than you and her? Not
My instinct, not at all, believing as I had that two lost
Souls had found each other. A thought that you had
Never entertained, that you dismissed, romantically naïve.

A quiet knock that came upon your garret door one
Night, a blue-eyed waif. You smiled at her and let
Her in, that constant twinkle in your eye, and gave
Her refuge from my impossible demands, her wayward
Trek to you as true as tulips turning toward the sun.

~

"Wow!" Erica said. "He really got you down, André."

118

"Himself, too," André answered without a hint of embarrassment.

"Did he describe the situation accurately, Paige?" Jocelyn asked.

"I guess so."

"You were a confused fugitive?" Erica asked.

"Yes. I'd been in Dayton with my parents, more into meditation than before, but not on Luke's level. And the fun of Frisco was still bobbing in my soul. And Luke had a one track mind toward becoming an initiator. He was impatient with my frivolity, but mainly bothered by my flirtatious nature."

"No more than flirtatious?" Erica asked.

Paige and Jocelyn exchanged glances.

"A little more, perhaps. André was hovering around, after all."

"Hovering?" André said. "I wouldn't put it quite like that."

"Wait a minute here," Erica persisted. "Paige, you mean you and André, while you were living with Luke."

Blushing, Paige said, "Well, once, if you really must know, Erica."

"Twice," André said.

"Well," Paige countered, "that second time at the movies...."

"Still counts," André said, "now that we're baring all."

"Poor, Luke," Erica said.

"Like you should talk," Paige answered.

"The point is," Jocelyn broke in, "you and Luke were in separate spheres at that time."

"Certainly sounds like it," Erica said. "On separate planets."

"Since when," Paige said, "have you earned the right to moralize?"

"I'm just saying."

"Come on, you two," André said.

"We're almost finished here," Jocelyn added, turning to Paige. "We're not talking morality at the moment."

"What are we talking?" Erica said.

"History," Jocelyn answered. "Let's leave it at that and finish up." She looked at Paige, who had shrunk back, hugging a pillow. "So, Paige, I respect you toughing all this out. Luke was still naively hoping to get back to what you two had first felt in Columbus, and you had moved on beyond that."

Paige scoffed, unusual for her. "Or sunk beneath it."

"Let's see your little toes, Paige," André said.

"Don't be silly," Jocelyn protested.

"No," André broke in. "Let's see them. My answer to Luke's question to me is, 'No, I never noticed her little toes."

"You do not have to show your toes, Paige," Jocelyn said.

"I don't mind," Paige answered bitterly. "Why don't we all strip naked and display all our flaws now that we're revealing everything." She pulled off her thin white socks, propped her heels on the edge of the coffee table and wiggled her toes.

"Geez," Jocelyn said despairingly. "No need for this show and tell."

"Luke's right," Erica said. "Little stubs."

"Son of a gun," André added. "Yeah – but cute."

"And what about the warm pudding, André?" Erica asked.

"Don't recall that. You liked my French toast, though, right, Paige?"

"I don't like your mocking me," she said, reaching for a tissue box.

"How long were you and Paige together, André?" Jocelyn asked.

"A month, maybe."

"I realized," Paige said with a hint of fervor, "how shallow my life was. Even André couldn't make it feel right. Luke's leaving me didn't seem like abandonment, but righteous condemnation. This may sound like ego, but I wasn't in the habit of being rejected. Except by Luke."

Erica began to say something, but Jocelyn immediately waved a hand to stop.

"So I went back to Dayton," Paige said, tugging her socks back on, "waited tables, saved money, meditated regularly, and went to Italy to an initiator training course. They'd moved to Italy from Spain."

"No new man in your life?" Jocelyn asked.

"Nothing steady."

"And that was the end of you and Luke?"

Though Paige knew she could stop here, she also knew that her stream of karma was flowing, which though disturbing, was a good thing. She was holding her own, not being devastated, handling it. So why not finish the job. Knowing she'd weathered the brunt of the storm, she lay the pillow aside, sat up straight and forged toward the finish line.

"No, Jocelyn, not quite the end. Fuji was this lovely little town in the mountains northeast of Rome, famous for its healing springs and mineral water, and one morning I was headed with some friends to a meeting and heard my name from across the plaza. I recognized Luke's voice immediately. And there he was, waving. He crossed over, and we talked. He'd decided to extend his stay with Maharishi."

"Wow," Jocelyn said. "Big surprise."

"Yes, I thought he'd finished in Spain. He was thrilled to see me, thought I'd finally seen the light."

"Any sparks along with that light?" André asked.

"Yes, there were always two way sparks between us. I always found him attractive. And in our off hours from training, we hung out in his room in a little pensionne, and in his training so far he'd learned the puja, and...."

"The puja?" Erica interrupted.

"Oh, sorry. A ritual used as part of the instruction into TM, a thanks to the tradition TM comes from, with some simple offerings, all in Sanskrit – very beautiful – and Luke demonstrated it. Showing off, I guess."

"And you were lovers once again?" Jocelyn asked.

Paige nodded. "Yes, but...."

"But what, Paige?"

"Well, I'd met someone else, on the charter flight from New York. And I knew Luke thought that he and I would be together, that I'd finally realized what we'd once had and now would have again, but it wasn't like that for me, and...."

"Had it ever been?" André asked.

Paige shook her head as if in remorse. "Maybe, for those first few months, when my head was swirling from all the intensity."

"Back to the elephant," André said. "What really happened between you two? What broke that feeling up?"

Without spirit, Paige looked knowingly at Jocelyn. "I guess I'd only been that horny housewife you mentioned yesterday, André. Never up to his vision of soul mates."

"Vision?" Erica said. "Or pure myth."

A moment of silence passed among them.

"I wish I knew," Paige finally said.

"Back to Italy," Jocelyn broke the mood.

Paige let out a sigh, part embarrassment, part fatigue. "And then the guy I'd met, Timothy, proposed to me and..."

"And?"

"And I accepted. You see, after Lancaster I realized I was not the one for Luke, that I'd keep breaking his heart over and over if he let me. I'd moved on, our paths had crossed, past tense, and I was falling in love with Timothy."

"And sleeping with him there in the bath town?" Erica asked.

"Yes, Erica, and after he proposed to me I saw a future ahead with him in Santa Fe, and stopped seeing Luke, and knew he was hurting terribly, but he'd been doing so well on the training course, I knew I'd only drag him down, and I was happy with Timothy, and couldn't handle both because we singles weren't really supposed to be doing any of this while on the course and...."

"So you washed your hands of Luke," Jocelyn said.

"I don't like to put it that way. The course ended for me, all I could afford. I'd become an initiator. Timothy and I went back to New Mexico and got married. Luke stayed in Italy for another advanced course, going ever more deeply into the teaching."

"End of the story of Luke and Diane. I mean Paige," André said. "Whose song was that about Luke and Diane?"

Paige rolled her eyes toward the ceiling as if to say with humiliation, *No, not the end of the story yet.*

"*Jack* and Diane," Erica said. "Not Luke."

"Billy Joel, right?" André asked.

"John Cougar Mellencamp."

"That's it. I have it on the juke. I'll play it later. But who was in the Billy Joel song?"

"Brenda and Eddie," Erica said.

"Right. Brenda and Eddie. I always get those two songs mixed up. And Bobby Joe and Billy Sue? – The ones that took the money and ran? Whose song was that?"

"*Billy* Joe and *Bobby* Sue," Erica said. "Steve Miller Band."

"Hey," Jocelyn interrupted. "We're way off the subject here."

By this time the wine was gone, the teacups empty, and the chocolates all consumed. The group stretched uneasily.

"Did you say there's more, Paige?" Jocelyn asked.

"Not much," Paige said. "Not that changed anything. Let's skip it."

"No, let's get it all on the table," Erica said. "No use leaving the theater before the final scene."

"Maybe we got the gist," André countered. "Why not let the poor girl off the hook?"

"I want to hear it," Erica insisted. "You guys can go to bed if you like, but we've come this far, I want to know how the story ends."

"I'll stick it out with you," Jocelyn said.

"I'm not one to desert a pal," André added. "Especially three of them, all ravishing." Then after puzzling a moment, he said, "Is that what I did with Luke. Desert a pal?"

Jocelyn gasped, clapped her hands.

"What," André said defensively.

"That's the first hint of introspection I've ever heard out of you."

"Okay, that's fine. Do the three of you think I did something wrong by being with Paige after Luke walked out on her?"

"No," Erica reacted immediately. "You were both adults. But didn't I hear a little while ago that it was *during* as well as after, something in a movie theater?"

"From the poem," Jocelyn added, "Luke seemed to have understood it – 'tulips turning toward the sun.' You needn't feel guilty, André, if guilt is actually what you're feeling."

"Well, I felt a little guilty after I got this poem, but certainly not way back when Paige knocked on my door. That was a no-brainer."

"That's right, André," Jocelyn said. "You would have done nothing else. And Paige had every reason to seek solace with a friend much more on her wave length. Luke knew it."

"The jury finds you 'Not Guilty,' André!" pronounced Erica with glee.

"Yeah," André said, "but it cost me Luke's friendship. He came to town, didn't feel he could call me, never kept in touch until this letter. I think I would have liked to keep contact, at least get together when he came home, give him a haircut, even answer his questions about Paige."

"He just wasn't like you, André," Jocelyn said. "But he recognized the difference, accepted it, looked up to you. No reason whatever for you to fret about it."

"Right," Erica added. "We like you just the way you are. A no-brooding zone."

"Anyway," Jocelyn said, "let's finish your story, Paige. You went to Santa Fe and got married to Timothy. Then what?"

"End of Luke and Paige?" Erica asked. "Final credits rolling?"

"Maybe a song someday," André said.

"Not quite the end, everyone, but let's leave it there, okay?"

"One more reference," Jocelyn said, "back in Luke's poem to *you*, Paige. What's the thing about Zuma Beach? You didn't explain that."

"Oh. Yes, Zuma was the end. That was a few years later, must have been nineteen seventy-seven."

"Okay," Erica said, bright eyed. "Let's hear it. Closure."

"All right. Luke had become a name in the movement. He'd gone from his Harrisburg center to being the coordinator for all the centers in New York State, then joined Maharishi's staff in Switzerland, and then on the board of our national headquarters in Los Angeles. I'd heard his name mentioned now and then, and always paid attention. After my breakup with Timothy, I contacted a friend of mine in Malibu to see if they needed anyone on staff at National, and they did, housekeepers, and I grabbed it. Room and board and a small salary."

"Luke was the top gun in meditation?" André asked.

"One of them. He managed things. Anyway, he happened to be living at National, which is why, when I was desperate, I took a job there."

"So it became your penance to clean his room?" Erica said, lying back, stretching her legs out.

"It might have, but I didn't go there for penance and didn't stay long. I wanted to see him again. I wondered if we might start over. I felt ready to lead a devout life with him, but...."

"Yes, Paige, go on," Jocelyn said. "Zuma Beach."

"All right, then, Zuma Beach..."

...flashback May, 1977

She stared at his hands on the steering wheel. She felt tight in her stomach, wondered if she should have come to see him. But he had always been her destination when she'd needed refuge. This time, however, it was more than refuge, much more.

He drove silently, his expression stern, focused on the busy highway through sunlight, shade from eucalyptus, vistas of the Pacific flashing by. His uneasiness told her that he still loved her. Six years had passed since she'd last seen him. That was in Italy.

On the beach at Zuma where they'd come to talk away from spying eyes at the National Center, she hoped he would hold her hand, but he maintained distance between them. Waves crashed, surfers riding them in, the scent of the sea, kelp-strewn sand, sun beating down.

"Do you have someone, Luke?"

She knew he didn't; she'd asked around.

"The work is all."

"I understand it now."

"Understand what?"

"What you were trying to tell me, back then. What you wanted to give me when I was so terribly stupid. What you wanted from me. I can give that to you now."

He glanced at her in the glare of the sun, pain, seeming derision in his eyes.

"I'd like so much for you to hold me," she said, grasping his hand.

"I can't."

"You said there was no one."

"It's you. It's always been you. But you're lost to me."

"Luke, I'm ready now. I see now. I know it took me so infinitely long, but I know what you meant in that incredible letter you sent me about the Gita. It was far over my dumb head back then, but I see it now. I'm there. Still have that letter. It's a treasure."

"Too much to forget, to forgive."

They were in front of boulders at the base of a cliff. She tugged his hand.

"Let's go into the shade. Hold me, dear Luke."

"No. I've found peace. I can't go back."

"You said once, during all our strife, that you would hold me in your heart like a seed to bloom again. Luke, that seed is ready. Once I saw it, once the light shone through my ignorance, I had to leave Timothy. There was only you. Please, Luke."

"Not again, Paige."

"Let me stay with you tonight, spend time with you. Then, you'll see. Then you'll trust me."

"I'm sorry. I've learned to live without you. I ... I can't trust you. Come on, let's go back. Nothing more to say."

In spite of the heat, a chill passed through her. He'd pushed her out, would not allow her back in. Of course. What could she expect? She knew about the Law of Karma, about personal responsibility, but she stung from his having blocked her out. She could not blame him, not a bit. And thanks to her growth in the Knowledge, she had the tools to cope. At least during the silent ride back to Malibu, she hoped so.

~

"I told him, Page said, "I finally understood what he'd always wanted, and I was ready for that, then he explained, with an agonized expression on his face, that he'd always been in love with me, that there'd never been anyone else, but...."

"You keep stopping short, Paige," Erica said with a tinge of cruelty.

Determined not to express anger at the very end, Paige looked at Erica and silently forgave her for her crudeness. "Yes. Sorry." She pulled some tissues from the box, dabbed her eyes.

"Please go on," Jocelyn said gently.

"That's enough. I'm finished. Just like Luke and I were, from that day."

"He was searching for Columbus snow," André noted, seeming proud to have remembered the reference in Luke's poem to her. "Sounds like he could have had it again."

"I was looking for that too, finally. I had never forgotten about those early days with him. He had really swept me up into his vision of ideal love ... for a while. I just hadn't been capable of it. Then he saw Maharishi's message of enlightenment. And I missed that too until far too late."

"So you cleaned house for him in Malibu?" Erica asked.

"No. I couldn't have stayed there. I knew he still loved me, the way we'd been at first in Ohio, before I..." – she glanced at Jocelyn – "went crazy, but back then I had to get out of Columbus. He was right about that." Finally, knowing she'd finished intact, she smiled, like someone limping to the end of a marathon but joyous to have reached the finish line. "So here's the quick wrap-up. I called a friend of mine in Des Moines, went there and happened to meet William at the TM center. We became a couple, got married, and moved to Fairfield where William is vice-president of the School of Advanced Management, and where I got my Ph.D. in Sanskrit and now teach."

"Luke out of your system?" Jocelyn asked.

"Yes, we're accredited," Paige said, too relieved for annoyance. "A few years later, I got an email from him. He left the movement, working on his doctorate in Delaware. He asked if I wanted to talk, and I wrote back that I'd transcended our past, that he should just look at us as two people whose paths had once crossed."

"That's putting it mildly," Erica said. "Closure, at last?"

"Until I got his poem. Until right now. All this karma hitting me like a firestorm. I lost track of him. Guess he moved to Florida."

"And wrote some parting letters," André said, "then committed suicide in his car."

They sat in silence a moment.

"No more closure than that," Erica said.

"And he died still loving you, Paige," André added.

"He never knew Paige," Jocelyn blurted. "He only knew a dream of something he felt he'd once had and lost, never knowing why. It was the not-knowing that must have been the hardest part. I guess it all came down to his question to you, André."

"What question is that?"

"Was his relationship with Paige as miraculous for her as it was for him, or was it merely like *you* and her?"

"Are you asking me?" André said in a rare defensive tone.

"Maybe we should ask Paige," Jocelyn answered. "Was it miraculous for you, Paige?"

"You're putting her on the spot," André said. "For me, Paige and I were miraculous, just like you and me, Joss, and just like Erica and me."

"And just like Muriel, I'm sure," Jocelyn answered. "For you, they're all miraculous. So I will ask Paige. Paige, who were you more at home with, happier with – you and Luke, or you and André? And you and Jesse, and how many others?"

In sudden horror, Paige stared at Jocelyn.

"Well?" Jocelyn asked sternly.

"At home with?" Paige said bitterly, suddenly finding herself held in judgement by her once confidante, "or miraculous. I guess I can say I'm not at home with miracles. Luke loved me the way I've never been loved before or since. He was at ease with miracles, had always believed in them, had thought the two of us had been blundering through life trying to find each other and finally had. For a little while, a few months, he convinced me of that. It was scintillating to be an object of that. But it became too much. That's all I can say. In the end, I couldn't live up to it. I'm flawed, Jocelyn, unlike you, apparently."

"Couldn't live up to the pressure of having to be ideal," Jocelyn said. "You were even willing to die to get out of that pressure."

"In his way, André *is* miraculous," Paige answered, giving him a weak smile.

"Like the sun," Erica said, "that we tulips turn toward."

Paige's smile brightened falsely. "Yes, Erica, like that."

They were silent again as if sanctifying André as the giver of light.

"Gonna play that song about Luke and Diane," he said, jumping up.

18

André's tap on the door wasn't loud enough to have awakened Jocelyn if she'd been asleep. But she wasn't asleep. She turned on the nightstand light, slid out of bed, pulled on a short robe and opened the door. He slipped inside.

"What is it, André?"

He pulled her into a hug, which she returned.

"Can we talk a minute?" he said softly.

"All right."

"Awake enough?"

"Yes, couldn't sleep. What is it?"

"Get in bed, I'll pull a chair up."

"No need," she said. "We can lie together."

"That sounds great."

"Don't get the *wrong* idea, André."

"Nothing *wrong* about it, but don't worry. You're in charge."

"Your women are always in charge, aren't they? That's what's so lovely about you."

Stretched out together, distance between them, the light still on, Jocelyn said, "Now what's on your mind, you dear man?"

"I want you to tell me what's wrong."

"What do you mean?"

"Come on. Out with it. You're not well."

"Well enough."

"You're very sick, aren't you, Joss?"

Their eyes locked in the dim light.

"Aren't you?" he persisted.

"You mustn't mention a word to the others, André."

"I promise. Now tell me."

"Pancreatic. Non operable."

After a moment of silence, still staring at each other, André said, "Come here, baby."

"Oh, André."

She moved into his arms. He held her close as she wept long and softly against his shoulder.

~

When Jocelyn woke in the dim morning light, André was sleeping soundly in his clothes. She jostled him, and he muttered something undiscernible. She touched his cheek tenderly.

"You'd better leave," she said.

In a moment he came to. "Uh, thing is..."

"We needn't say more."

"Maybe we needn't, but may I?"

"All right."

"Just the last thing, nothing else."

"Say it then."

"Maybe you won't like it."

"I'm a psychoanalyst, André. Whatever is on your mind?"

"Okay. It's just that ... well, here it is. I know you haven't gotten over Tony. Not even after all these years."

She took a startled breath, didn't know how to respond.

André went on. "I know that ... you and Luke believed in the same thing, and always have."

"Stop it, André. Don't make me cry again."

"Just that you've always thought I just slide along on the surface, but..."

"But what?"

"But, I don't, Joss. I see. I feel."

"All right, André."

"And I do understand how you felt about Tony, and how Luke felt about Paige."

"Really?"

"It's what we all want, isn't it? I'm no different, not a bit."

"Who was *your* Grand Passion with, André?"

"All of you. Each one. It's just that..."

"Just that what, you jewel of a man?"

"It's just that, no one ever stayed."

~

After another of Caroline's scrumptious morning meals, Jocelyn drove them all to the small Lancaster airport to see Paige off.

"Sorry I was snide to you," Erica said.

"My karma," Paige answered, smiling truly. "Payment fully made."

One by one, she hugged them all. Thankful to be departing and free of a burden, she left them standing at the security checkpoint.

The remaining trio took a circuitous drive westward into the countryside across the Susquehanna at Columbia after which they followed the river southward to Otter Creek, a tributary that rushed over boulders into whirlpools and falls. Others, young and sleek, dived from a rope and plunged into the water, their shouts and laughter echoing into the forest. Erica and André joined them in the stream as Jocelyn found a sunny rock and let the current wash over her legs.

Later that afternoon Erica drove off to spend the night at her daughter's house and to head to Harrisburg next morning for her flight to Chicago and onward to Seattle.

Jocelyn and André spent their remaining time together going through André's extensive sketches, designs, paintings and sculptures.

In his studio, several works in progress, he said, "Why don't you move in with me, Joss? Plenty of room, back here to your roots."

"Oh, no. That's very kind. But I've put down very deep roots back in the City, and I have lots of loose ends to tie. But stay with me tonight, dear André. I so love your holding me. Let's do that one more night before I go."

End

OTHER BOOKS by JON MICHAEL MILLER

Available in print or eBook at amazon.com/author/jonmichaelmiller

MAHARISHI, TM, MALLORY & ME: Echoing *Five Paths Crossing*, this memoir traces Miller's early years and his twelve-year involvement in the Transcendental Meditation Movement as led by Maharishi Mahesh Yogi, famous guru of the Beatles, the Beach Boys, and many other celebrities. TM's benefits are now often touted by Jerry Seinfeld. Also, a complex love story.

LOVE and WAR at KENT STATE: Miller's masterpiece, this historical novel depicts the step-by-step buildup to and including those final tragic days in May, 1970, when the Ohio National Guard gunned down unarmed students at Kent State University. Experience it from the perspective of a passionate love story of two grad students trying to find themselves and to forge their careers in the midst of the madness.

GOOD GIRLS, BAD GIRLS – Coming of Age in the 60s: A country boy, Jake Ernst grows up in an age of innocence compared to present days of hard drives, social media and ubiquitous porn. His mom tells him, "There are good girls and bad girls. Stay away from the bad ones." But what baffles Jake is, how does a guy tell one from the other? Jake is the precursor to the protagonist in *Love and War at Kent State*.

ROZ – The Story of a Jamaican Lolita: Miller's best seller. Roz is an impoverished island teen hell bent on capturing her prince charming, an unsuspecting, middle-aged tourist from America. This thrilling, comic romp takes you from one end of Jamaica to the other, better than a guided tour. Adult reading.

DRIFTWOOD HOUSES – A Key West Story Sequence: This spicy story collection presents saucy tales of local folks trying comically, ironically, to fulfill their dreams. With compassion, humor and slice of life realism, Miller's *tour de force* demonstrates his skill at presenting a diverse cast of characters.

MURDER & MAYHEM in TROPIC GARDENS: In this satirical murder mystery in a Florida retirement community, an ex-CIA researcher is plagued with unusual happenings and suspicious people, disrupting his highly coveted quiet life. He craves simplicity but discovers that a peaceful retirement is damned hard to find.

PHOTO SESSIONS – *Penn State Calendar Girls*: In this tongue-in-cheek novel of middle-aged madness, a college advisor seeking the erotic excitement of his youth turns to studio photography as a means of meeting beautiful young women. He soon discovers the folly as well as the danger of such an idea when his life is turned upside-down by the prospect of a long prison term.

CLOSE ENCOUNTERS of the JAMAICAN KIND: Set in Jamaica and in St. Pete, Florida, the protagonist of *Photo Sessions,* camera in hand, resumes his frantic quest for romantic fulfillment in a self-banishment from his earlier life. 'Close Encounters' is the name of a former flamboyant nightclub in Negril. He suffers the joys and the anguish of his quest. For adult readers.

NEGRIL BEACH – *Two Stories of Jamaica*: This duet of tales is set at one of the most beautiful and freewheeling beaches in the world. In one story, Ivor, a local beach hustler, takes on a mission from a tourist that comically tests his procurement skills to the limit. In the other, a dying American journalist faces his last days in the place he loves best.

The *VIRGIN, VIV*: In a time before laptops, cellphones, and HIV, three strangers meet, wrangle and grow. In a campus setting, we share their interdependent voyage with humor, confession, anguish, and personal evolution. We laugh with them, worry, and rejoice as their voices rise from the pages. They become simply unforgettable.

THROWN TOGETHER – *A Story of Love in Turbulent Times*: In this intense novel, a just-returned Vietnam soldier enters grad school and soon finds himself in a new conflict, entwined in a passionate love affair with a beautiful, floundering housewife. During the turmoil of the late sixties, their relationship leads them across the continent and forges new identities.

amazon.com/author/jonmichaelmiller

~~

Made in the USA
Columbia, SC
18 September 2023

22932404R00086